With best wishes,
C. R. [signature]

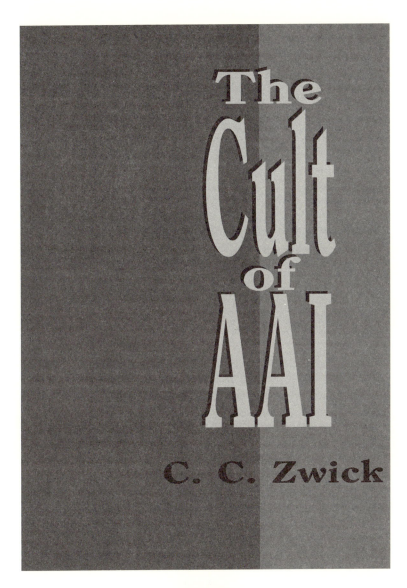

The Cult of AAI

C. C. Zwick

Pentland Press, Inc.
England•USA•Scotland

PUBLISHED BY PENTLAND PRESS, INC.
5122 Bur Oak Circle, Raleigh, North Carolina 27612
United States of America
(919)782-0281

ISBN: 1-57197-146-7
Library of Congress Catalog Card Number 98-068265
Copyright © 1999 C. C. Zwick
All rights reserved, which includes the right to reproduce this book or portions thereof in any form whatsoever except as provided by the U.S. Copyright Law.
Printed in the United States of America

If only you would destroy the wicked, O God, and the men of blood were to depart from me;
Do I not hate, O Lord, those who hate you? Those who rise up against you do I not loathe?
With a deadly hatred I hate them; they are my enemies.
—Psalms, 138: 19, 21, 22

Part One

Chapter 1

I had never liked the man. I must say this at the outset. He was considerably overweight and he possessed those obnoxious qualities that seem to characterize certain obese people. He was loud-mouthed—a trait I particularly detest—profane in his speech more than was necessary, and brusque to the point of rudeness. He also had an eye for the ladies, if I may use that timeworn expression. I am not a prude in that respect, but it seems to me that when a man reaches his middle years he ought to taper off a little, act his age, direct his inclinations to, well, elderly pursuits, whatever they may be.

Anyway, you get the picture. George Weston was a disagreeable person, and few of his co-workers enjoyed associating with him. As luck would have it, I had been assigned a desk adjoining his when I began my employment in the accounting department of Smith and Holmes Department Store, and being something of a straitlaced, modest fellow, I soon found myself becoming the butt of his tactless, off-color remarks.

I thought often of quitting those first few weeks. It was not in my nature to answer him in kind. Perhaps this would have put an end to his infernal badgering. However, I don't think it would have succeeded. His type always seems to lack the sensibility that permits an evaluation of one's own shortcomings. The

George Westons of this world simply do not realize how obnoxious they can be.

Since this was my very first job and I needed the money, I decided reluctantly to stick it out for a while, gain a little experience, then look for employment elsewhere, hopefully improving myself in the process.

Strangely enough, as the weeks went by, there was a remarkable change in the man's attitude toward me. The barbs grew fewer and fewer and eventually disappeared altogether. The change occurred so gradually that I was hardly aware of it at first. I don't mean to say that the man's personality changed; he remained as disgusting as ever. Nor was there any friendship developing between us, for it would have been difficult to imagine two people more totally unlike, he being fat and fiftyish, divorced or widowed, ill-tempered, and ill-mannered, while I was in my early twenties, quite serious and industrious, and doggedly determined to be amiable with one and all. (I was, incidentally, romantically unattached at the time and not too inclined to alter that position until my finances greatly improved.)

The change came about as a result of a topic of conversation that Weston seemed determined to pursue. He had begun, as I recall, by making disparaging remarks concerning the church with which I was affiliated and to Christianity in general. At first I ignored his rantings as typical of the man and I refused to be drawn in on such a touchy subject. After all, better minds than mine have argued the validity of the Christian doctrine. Gradually, however, I began to interject a point here and there, timidly in the beginning so I wouldn't arouse his ire or promote a general office debate. My first attempts at rebuttal were, I am sure, crude and naïve, as any lay person's would naturally be, and they produced the effect I feared most—arousing him to further heretical abuse.

I will admit that he made some valid statements that I found impossible to refute. On one occasion, I recall, when the question of slavery had been bandied about the office for several minutes—how inhuman it was, and how the blacks had been oppressed in this country for 200 years and for thousands of years before that—someone made a rather inane observation that it was over and done with, and that the Church, thank God, had helped abolish this hideous practice.

"The Church!" Weston guffawed. "The Church, did you say? What did the Church ever do to stop slavery? There was more slavery during the Middle Ages when the Church was in power than at any time in history. For Christ sake, the Church made slaves of everyone with their goddamn laws, slaves in mind as well as body."

The silence that followed this outburst should have told Weston that he had made his point, and no one wished to pursue it further. He was not so observant, however. He had warmed to his subject now, and nothing could stop him.

"I'll tell you something else," he continued heatedly, "something you religious fanatics completely ignore. You think you know something about slavery? Slavery has always existed. It's as old as mankind. And I can quote a passage from your damned Bible which shows that your noble God not only knew about slavery but condoned it as well!"

No one dared utter a word. Perhaps each of us waited for someone else to offer a response.

"You don't believe me?" Weston insisted. "Well, get out your Bible and look in the first book. Look in chapter seventeen of Genesis, read about Abraham, how God told him, 'He that is eight days old among you shall be circumcised, every male throughout your generations, including the slave born in your house, or bought with money from any foreigner, not of your own race.'

"So these chosen people, as they like to call themselves, these Jews, who have had their fill of slavery down through the years, practiced slavery even among themselves, and their great Jehovah approved of it as well!"

Needless to say, none of us had an answer for this. As I remember, a gloomy silence descended on the entire office, as if all of us had been trapped in our own guilt.

On another occasion, a news report of some brutal murders committed the day before by local teenagers induced a general indictment of today's young people and their preoccupation with drugs, sex, and violence. As luck would have it, someone brought Christ into the picture. "We need a return to Christ," this woman suggested. "Christ would put these kids in their place." Then someone blundered even further, calling Christ a man of questionable character, consorting with prostitutes and other sinners, living like a hippie, challenging the authorities. Weston had been strangely silent throughout this discussion, as if waiting for the proper moment to plunge in. When someone argued that Christ was hardly the hippie type, that he was a man of peace with the highest regard for everyone, Weston exploded.

"Baloney!" he bellowed. "Have you forgotten how he drove the merchants out of the temple? I'd say this was a pretty violent form of protest."

"Well," I countered meekly, "there was a reason for his violence, as you call it, on that occasion. He was protesting the use of the temple as a market place."

"Reason or not, what he did was no different from the rock throwings and dormitory burnings practiced by college kids in the sixties."

"I don't want to argue the point," I said. "Maybe you're right. I don't know. But this is the only time he gave way to anger, and we can excuse him for that."

"You mean, this is the only time that's been recorded," Weston countered. "How many other times were that there that you know nothing about? How about the times he cursed the Jewish leaders and called them hypocrites?

"Another thing. You call Christ a man of peace. How about the night he was taken prisoner in Gethsemane and Peter cut off the ear of one of the guards? If Christ was a man of peace, why was his chief apostle carrying a sword?"

Again there was silence following this outburst. No one was inclined to argue with him. He was too well versed in his subject for any of us to offer any kind of rebuttal.

The weeks went by with frequent and violent outbursts from Weston. And always, the aftermath was a dead, defeated silence. The man was evidently a fanatic on the subject of religion, and he had arguments that seemed irrefutable.

Gradually, however, I was able to draw on my early religious training to give him some pause for thought. I suppose it is difficult for the most violent of men to continue in anger when there is no opposition. I seemed to have a calming effect on him. When he ridiculed the creation of the world as described in Genesis, I merely informed him that the Bible was never intended as a book of science, that it was written in the vernacular of the time with the limited knowledge of the time. For the author of Genesis to have described the creation of the universe in the words of a modern astronomer or physicist would have been impossible. It also would have been unintelligible to early readers.

Weston seemed rather pleased with my explanation, and in the weeks that followed, our discussions continued on a saner level. Of course, I had no hope of converting him. He was much too anti-Christian for that. However, he grew amazingly patient at hearing me out and seemed ready to consider my arguments.

The more we discussed the matter—he seemed obsessed with this particular subject—the closer we appeared to be drawn together. Perhaps, I thought at first, he really wants to believe in God and he is hoping I can come up with the answers he needs. I gradually realized my mistake, however. He despised God thoroughly. No arguments of mine would ever change his mind. Why this simulated friendship then? Was the man lonely for companionship? Did he welcome the few crumbs of kindness I threw his way? No, there was nothing in our relationship to remotely suggest the possibility of any close ties. The entire association revolved around our debates concerning Jesus Christ, whom he ridiculed and whom I defended as the true son of the creator of the universe.

So it was with a great deal of surprise that I found myself confronted with an awkward decision one Friday afternoon. Weston invited me to spend an evening at his home. I had casually mentioned that I had no plans for the weekend, and his offer caught me completely off guard. I found myself accepting even as I was protesting to myself, and politely to him, that I didn't want to get involved in any office relationships. Weston and I had absolutely nothing in common. What could have possessed me to acquiesce to this middle-aged, ill-mannered, argumentative man?

Chapter 2

Weston lived quite some distance out of the city, beyond the suburbs. At every bend of the road, at each additional mile, I questioned my motives and wanted to turn back. Still, I drove on, drawn by some irrational urge I couldn't seem to resist.

It was nearly nine o'clock when I pulled into his driveway. In the twilight of this spring evening I could see that Weston had done very well for himself. The gray frame house was large and well tended, lodged amid magnificent pines and oaks. Apparently he was a man of considerable means.

He greeted me warmly at the door, graciously invited me in, seeming pleased that I had come. He assured me that I wasn't late. Dinner was ready to be served.

The house was tastefully furnished and bespoke a woman's touch in its appearance and cleanliness. I had come prepared for — well, anything. The man had always seemed so coarse and brutish that the charm and character of this house made me wonder if we had misjudged him, perhaps even induced the attitude he presented to us by our showing such dislike toward him.

I was further surprised when, upon being ushered into the dining room, I found the table set for three, and the final arrangements being made by the third person herself, whom Weston immediately introduced as his daughter, Joanne.

I had said previously that I was romantically unattached. I am prepared now to retract that statement. If it is possible to fall in love at first sight, Joanne Weston produced that emotion in me. She was about nineteen years old, boyishly slim as girls are today, with a heart-shaped face framed in long brown tresses. I could have kicked myself then and there for ever having questioned my decision to come.

The thought occurred to me that perhaps Weston had had this in mind when he extended his invitation. Did he consider me a suitable prospect for his daughter? It was just a passing thought, and I dismissed it almost immediately. Fathers don't do that anymore, do they? Besides, this girl would never lack for suitors, that was for sure.

As for Joanne, I must say, except for a quick, almost flushed reaction to our introduction, she was apparently not too eager to encourage any friendship. There was something, some invisible barrier, that sprang up immediately between us, a wall I could not understand or penetrate. On the whole she seemed friendly enough, a charming and gracious hostess. At times I even detected a hint of some return of my obvious admiration. She was quick to cover it, however. Or was I just imagining everything?

The meal was tastefully prepared and pleasant throughout. When it was over, I complimented Weston and his daughter.

"Joanne does it all," Weston explained proudly, "the cooking, cleaning, everything. And very well, too."

"Mother passed away two years ago," Joanne volunteered.

What was it? Sadness? Loneliness? Yes, but something a little more in her expression. Did the corners of her mouth turn down grimly as she glanced at her father?

"I'm sorry to hear that," I said.

"Yes, she does it all," Weston went on thoughtlessly. "You know, we men are no good at that sort of thing."

"You're lucky to have such a—" I checked myself then. I was about to say . . . what? Wonderful? Lovely? "—big help," I concluded. It was all I dared say at the moment.

She was quiet during the latter part of this exchange. Not embarrassed really, but thoughtful and indifferent, as if her mind had strayed elsewhere. Was she as conscientious as her father described, or merely fulfilling some family obligation? I began to wonder about this girl, living with this man for a father. She seemed modest and restrained by comparison. Was this an act for my benefit? Did she share her father's views on God and religion? I stole a glance at her and was astonished to see what I had not noticed before, a tiny gold crucifix at her throat, suspended by a gold chain.

"Well," said Weston suddenly, getting up, "I suppose we men can retire while Joanne cleans up."

I protested. This was unthinkable, letting this poor girl do all the work. "Let me help," I offered. "I'll be glad to help."

"Nonsense!" Weston exploded. "You're the guest here. Besides, Joanne does this all the time. Don't you, Joanne? You come with me, John. I want to show you something."

"Really," I said to Joanne, "I'd be glad to give you a hand."

"Thank you, but it's no bother. I can manage. You had better go with my father."

"This way," Weston said.

Joanne gave me a look that said, Go on. Go with him.

Clearly, something was wrong here. Why this curt dismissal? Did she mean that I had business with her father which excluded her? That had to be it. I wanted to explain to her that this was a casual visit, that I had come merely as a friend. Or was this the case? Did Weston have some purpose in mind, something the girl knew perhaps from past occasions?

"Well, okay," I muttered. I could think of nothing else to say.

"Through here," Weston directed.

I gave the girl one last despairing look. The expression on her face—what was it? Sickened? Disgusted? What was going on here? She seemed attracted to me. Nevertheless, I had the impression that I also repelled her.

Chapter 3

"Sit down, John," Weston said graciously. "Let me get you a drink. What do you like, brandy? Scotch?" We were in a small room just off the living room, a sort of den, with book-lined walls, a cluttered desk, a few leather chairs.

"No, thanks. I'll smoke, if you don't mind." I offered him a cigarette, but he declined. Weston took his time mixing a drink for himself while I sat down and surveyed the room. I'll say this for Weston, whatever kind of man he was, he certainly lived well.

"So," he began, seating himself opposite me and enjoying a sip. "This is my study. I spend a lot of evening hours here, reading, writing. I do research on several subjects. Religion, mostly. Religions of the world. They're all basically alike, you know."

I didn't know. I let him proceed. I supposed he was leading up to something.

"Christianity, Judaism, Islam, Buddhism, Shintoism—whatever you want to call it. One god, or many gods, living gods, dead gods, spirits, idols."

"None of which you believe in," I suggested.

"None of those I believe in," he corrected me. "But you are wrong. I do have a god." He took another drink from his glass. "If you want to call him that."

I remained silent. This was his scene. Let him read the lines.

"Your god is dead, you know," he said.

"Wha-a-at?" I blurted out, laughing.

"It's true. Look around you. Christianity is dying out. It's finished. You are losing your clergy. Your nuns are rebelling, demanding more participation. Without schools, how will your Church survive?"

"The Church will always survive. It has survived many crises."

"That old line?" Weston laughed. "'I will be with you always.' That's rot. Baloney. Christ was a fraud. Your theologians know it. They are doing their damnedest to defend the Bible against the realities of modern science. Take the virgin birth, for instance. A physical impossibility. Only ancient dummies could have believed that yarn."

"You just said the magic word. Physical. This was a spiritual event."

"Spiritual? Wake up, will you, boy? You're talking utter nonsense. This was a live birth. How could it be spiritual?

"Besides, have you read your Bible lately? Have you read your 'now' translation? For two thousand years your Bible proclaimed the virgin birth of Mary's only son. Mary was a virgin all her life, right? What does your Bible say now? Now your Bible admits that Christ had brothers and sisters. So there is one dogma thrown out the window right there!"

I was suddenly very irritated and got to my feet.

"George," I said, trying to be patient, "Look, I appreciate your inviting me here. I had a very nice dinner. You have a wonderful daughter and I was happy to meet her. But we have been arguing religion every day of every week for six months, and I'm filled up to here. If this is why you invited me here, to continue this insane discussion, well, forget it. I'm just not in the mood anymore."

Weston heard me out with equal patience. He looked down at his almost finished drink, swishing the ice around on the bottom before answering.

"Yes," he admitted finally, "you're right. I have gone overboard, haven't I? Sorry about that. But you're wrong. I didn't ask you here to start another debate. Actually I wanted to show you something. That is, if you're still interested."

"Interested? Interested in what? Has this something to do with what we've been discussing?"

"Well, yes, as a matter of fact, it does."

He drained his glass and began to mix another.

"Are you sure you don't want something?" he asked. "You may need it."

"No, thanks." He had certainly aroused my curiosity now. What did he mean, I might need one?

Weston took a long sip before continuing. "I said a few minutes ago that I have a god. Well, I do, and many more like me do, too. And there are countless millions who worship this god without realizing it. The list might even include you, John."

I had a sudden thought and let it fly. "Are you by any chance referring to the devil?"

Weston shrugged. "The devil, Satan, Lucifer, Beelzebub, Baal, anything you want to call him."

I didn't know whether to be amused or disgusted. "Do you mean to tell me that you belong to a cult of devil worshippers?"

"You find this shocking? Perhaps you consider it a big joke, eh? A group of idiots playing make believe, perverts letting out their inhibitions, acting out their fantasies? Well, let me assure you, this is no joke."

I found it hard to believe. "You actually worship the devil?"

He gave me a weary smile. "You know, John, you Christians are something else. You really are. You say you believe in God. Why? Because your Bible tells you there is a god. Your Bible also tells you there is a devil. But do you believe in the devil?" Weston snorted. "No. To you the devil is a big joke, a Middle Ages boogeyman, a character in your horror movies. You're so full of this Christ worship you can't imagine that hell or the devil exist."

"I don't think that's true. We've been taught to believe that Christ saved us and we don't think of anything but going to heaven."

"Saved you!" Weston laughed. "Saved you from what? Saved you from the kind of life man was meant to live? This goody-goody life Christ lived, what good did it do him?"

"He triumphed over it, didn't he?"

The Cult of AAI

"Are you Christ? Is everybody a Christ? Besides, what proof do you have that Christ came back to life? Just your damned Bible that's a pack of falsehoods!"

"George, are we back to that again? I thought we were going to drop that subject."

"I have no intention of getting back on that subject. I am merely trying to convince you that there is a world I believe in other than your heaven, a god who is as great as your god, who has endured as long as your god."

"Wasn't your god created by my God?"

"That is what your Bible would have you believe."

"Well, if we can't believe the Bible, which is the direct word of God, what can we believe?"

"All truth is not contained in the Bible. All knowledge is not held in the Bible."

"Oh, I grant you that. Mathematics, astronomy, chemistry, archaeology . . ."

Weston held up a hand. "Please, John, no jokes? Give me that consideration at least, will you?"

I got to my feet. "George, it's getting late. I have a long drive back to town. Why don't we call it an evening?"

Weston agreed. "But I promised to show you something. I want you to see this."

Were we back to that again? "Okay, but make it fast, will you?"

He turned to an inner wall of the room, moved a picture aside to reveal a safe. He withdrew a glass case roughly two inches square. Holding it in the palm of his hand, he removed the cover and presented the bottom for my inspection. It held a single piece of rock, egg-shaped, about an inch long, greenish-black.

"What is it?" I asked.

"Look closely. Take a good look."

I moved to within a foot of his hand. The stone seemed more glossy now, with a bit of reddish color in the center. I am no lover of rare gems. The largest diamond in the world would not interest me greatly.

"Keep looking," Weston urged.

Keep looking? What was I supposed to be looking for?

C. C. Zwick

As I looked I thought I saw a movement in the stone, a shift of the reddish-orange color. Had there been a change in the reflection of the light? No. Weston was holding the stone steady. The color did move! Was I seeing things? It flickered like the flame of a candle. Of course it was an optical illusion. As I said earlier, I know nothing about minerals. Perhaps some stones do produce that effect.

"What is it? I asked, looking up at Weston.

He was actually jubilant in possession of his prize.

"That, my dear boy, is a living, breathing flame from hell!"

Chapter 4

Of course I laughed at Weston.
"Do I have to spell it out for you?" he insisted. "It's a fire from hell."

I wasn't ready to take him literally. "You mean, it's some kind of rare gem?"

Now his face reddened with exasperation. "John, listen to me, and listen well. Forget gems, forget anything you know about anything.

"What I'm telling you is this, here is a fire from another world. Do you see it flickering? Do you see that no matter how I turn or twist my hand, no matter how I place it in the light, it continues to burn freely and steadily?"

That put it in a language anyone could understand.

I bent down for a closer look. I still wasn't ready to accept his explanation, but I couldn't let skepticism waste this opportunity to debunk another of his skewed perceptions.

"Aren't you even remotely convinced?" he asked. "Here, let me turn off the light."

He flipped a wall switch, extinguishing the overhead fixture. However, we were not in total darkness as considerable light was reflected into the room from the hallway. George turned his back in that direction, holding the stone in the shadow of his chest.

"Now what do you see?" he demanded.

I looked and saw. If such a thing was possible, there was a fire, very small, like the flame of a birthday candle.

"Can I touch it?" I asked.

"By all means."

I put out my right forefinger gingerly. If there was a fire the stone ought to be pretty hot. It wasn't. It wasn't even warm. It felt like any other smooth stone. I let my finger lay on it. I added my thumb and second finger. I even lifted it slightly, almost deciding to palm it. I felt nothing.

"I see you aren't convinced yet."

"Well, you have to admit, where there's fire . . ."

"Exactly!" Weston exclaimed. He extended his right hand and the room was lit as before. "If this were an earthly fire the stone would be unbearably hot. Right? But you felt nothing. Let me also point out that this flame is completely enclosed, embedded in solid stone. Which makes it a physical impossibility. How can there be combustion without air?"

"That's right," I agreed.

"You think that proves your point?" Weston asked. "My boy, let me assure you, this stone has been examined by experts with the best scientific tools. It is solid, it is unbreakable. This is no gimmick, this is no trick. You recall the story of Moses in Exodus, the bush that was on fire but was not consumed? This is that fire. You see it right here before your eyes."

"Okay," I said. "So it's a fire from hell. So what? Where did you get it?" I was of course still unconvinced. "What are you doing with it?"

"Aha!" Weston grinned. "Now we come to the crux of the matter."

He replaced the cover and returned the box to the safe. Then he mixed himself another drink, and one for me, which I suddenly felt in need of, and sat down opposite me.

"John," he began, "I asked you here for a purpose. First, I wanted to show you proof of what I have to offer. Second, I like you. I like the way you stand up for what you believe in. We need people like you. I want you to join us."

"Us?" I repeated. "This cult of devil worshippers? The Black Mass and all that screwy bit?"

Weston waved a hand deprecatingly. "John, please! The Black Mass? Give us credit for some intelligence, will you? We are a civilized organization of sane human beings. Our only purpose is the worship of the true god of the universe."

"Satan?" I sneered.

"Whatever you wish to call him. He has as many names as there are tongues of speech. To us he is known as AAI."

I repressed a laugh. "Aye-eye?"

"AAI."

We were both silent for a minute. Weston seemed lost in a spiritual reverie. I, of course, had much to think about. Worship the devil? Give up all my ideals, my hope for eternity? Forget God, give up heaven? For what? Some crazy idea that the devil ruled the universe?

"I dunno, George," I said at last. "You show me a hunk of rock that may or may not be what you say it is, you ask me to give up everything I believe in, everything that's good and noble and true. For what? What would I get out of it? What good has it done you?"

"I hardly expected you to agree right away. I want you to think about it. Will you at least do that? We'll discuss this again. Meanwhile I have an important . . ." he paused briefly, as if searching for the right word, " . . . meeting this weekend. Next time we'll discuss this further."

He stood up, giving me occasion to leave. I got to my feet also. We shook hands, almost as if we were sealing a bargain.

Join him? I hardly thought so. Think about it? Only negatively. I was not about to join some secret organization that was involved in occult practices.

He led me to the door. I hoped to see his daughter again. I wanted to check my first impression. Was she as wonderful as I imagined? Was I mistaken about the crucifix at her throat?

Weston read my thoughts. "Joanne!" he called.

She appeared in the dining room doorway, but came no further.

"John is leaving," her father told her.

Yes, she was as lovely as I remembered, but that look of disgust, of — what was it? abhorrence? — was still on her face.

"Thanks for the dinner," I said. "I really enjoyed it."

"Thank you," she said in return, her tone emotionless.

"I'm very glad to have met you." I wanted to add that I hoped we would meet again, but the look on her face precluded that.

"John will be visiting us again," Weston told her.

"Oh, of course," was all she said.

"Well, goodnight," I said and stepped out.

George stood in the doorway, blocking my view of his daughter.

"Think about it, will you, John?" he asked. "Give it some serious thought. We'll discuss it later."

"Okay, George," I promised. "Goodnight."

He was still standing in the doorway as I drove off.

Chapter 5

I did considerable thinking over the weekend, but it was Joanne who occupied all my thoughts. Joanne. What a lovely girl she was. I had to meet her again. I had to talk to her, sound her out. I had to solve the paradox that existed in that house, this seemingly Christian child living with a man seriously dedicated to evil. And I was certain that what he was mixed up in was evil.

Devil worship? Perhaps I was naïve, but could anything good come of that? Wasn't it a mere excuse for orgies of the flesh, for villainous pursuits, for the overthrow of moral society? There are devils, I admitted, if religious authorities say so, but they are bound up by the power of God, not to be invoked or toyed with. And that stone of Weston's—what kind of trickery was that? It had to be false. How could such a thing exist in a material world?

I had no desire therefore to join Weston and his insane organization. Still, I was faced with this dilemma: if I wanted to see his daughter again, I had to visit her father again. Of course there was always the opportunity of phoning her. I even looked up Weston's number, but I could not bring myself to call her. As I said before, I am something of a straitlaced fellow, not timid, you understand, but not overly aggressive either. Besides, she had shown such obvious dislike or disinterest that any advance of mine at this stage was certain to be rebuffed.

I decided to wait until Monday. I would see Weston then. He was certain to bring up the membership matter, and I could sound him out on a few other things.

I was disappointed, however. Weston did not show up at work. No one seemed able to explain his absence. Naturally, rumors flew fast and furious. There were off-color jokes about him shacking up with some broad over the weekend. Others hoped he had contracted a terminal illness or resigned.

He was still absent on Wednesday, and no one knew why. On Thursday I became a little apprehensive. Was he sick, or had something gone wrong in one of his occult practices? Someone suggested that, since I had been on good terms with him, I should give him a call. I could not bring myself to do it. Perhaps I was still afraid of getting involved in something I could not escape. I realized I was missing an excellent opportunity. There was a chance that Joanne would answer the phone and I could renew, even enlarge, our acquaintanceship. But, as I said, I could not bring myself to do it. Perhaps I had a hunch, a premonition, that the matter would resolve itself with no initiative on my part.

When Weston did not show up on Friday there was little concern at the office. Everyone seemed agreed on his resignation or dismissal. I didn't know whether to be happy or disappointed at the way things had turned out. I was rid of Weston and his insane proposal, but on the other hand I had probably lost any chance of relating with his daughter.

I returned to my apartment after work—I lived alone—and spent the first part of the evening desultorily trying to interest myself in a number of boring things, television, the newspaper, a magazine. I was actually in a confused frame of mind. A world of plans had all but collapsed.

Around nine o'clock the phone rang. I jumped to answer it. The voice at the other end was Weston's. He greeted me eagerly. No, he hadn't been sick. He had taken a week's leave of absence. He had wanted to call earlier but was deeply involved in some research. He asked if I had done any thinking on his proposal and wondered if I would be interested in attending a meeting the following night.

"What is this going to be, some kind of Black Mass?" I couldn't keep the contempt out of my voice.

"John," he said exasperatedly, "I told you we don't go in for that sort of thing. That's a throwback to the Middle Ages. This is the twentieth century. This is the real thing. We are followers of the devil because we believe in him, because we have proof of his existence, and because we know he offers man everything he wants to make him happy in this world."

"Well," I stalled, trying to make up my mind, "where is this meeting going to be, at your place?"

"No. Tell you what you do, John. You drive out here and you can go with me."

It was the chance I'd hoped for, the chance to see Joanne again.

"Well, okay, but I want it understood, George, I'm going as a spectator. I don't want to get involved, not just yet at least, until I know what I'm getting into."

"Sure, sure." Weston was very sympathetic. "That's all I expect you to do. I want you to be convinced — and you will be tomorrow night — before you commit yourself."

"All right, then. I'll be there."

"Good," said Weston. "Try to be here about eight o'clock, will you?"

Needless to say, the next twenty-four hours were the most apprehensive of my life. Over and over I asked myself, what was I doing getting mixed up in this crazy business? I had been brought up in a Christian home; I was a faithful attendant at Sunday services; I felt deeply that a return of religious values was needed to bring the world back to decency and morality. Why was I getting mixed up with Weston and his devilish group?

Of course, there was only one answer. Joanne. I had become as obsessed with her as her father was with his damnable cult. To reach the daughter I had to play along with the father.

All my hopes were to be dashed, however. Joanne did not appear. Weston met me at the door, and after a short wait while he "got a few things together," we left in his car. The ride took the better part of an hour through a quickly descending dusk and over various country roads. I had no idea where we were or where we were heading. Weston himself was noncommittal, alone in his thoughts. We exchanged a few pleasantries about nothing in particular. Once, I know, I asked about Joanne.

"She's fine," he answered, "just fine."

I had a dozen questions I wanted to ask. Was she in college? Was she working? What did she do for relaxation? I could not bring myself to inquire. Weston seemed unwilling to pursue any subject.

It was dark when we pulled up at a rambling farm house. There were many cars already parked inside the rustic fence. The house, although well lit, was strangely quiet. Clearly this was a gathering for some serious purpose and in no sense of the word a party of amiable friends. Once inside, I found myself being introduced to fifty or more people. They were all adults of both sexes, names and faces all running together, so that soon I had no specific recollections. I will say that this was no motley gathering of abnormal characters. They were an intelligent-looking lot, drawn from the better walks of life. Chalk up one for Weston and his organization.

Perhaps thirty minutes went by. We gathered in little groups, exchanging small talk about the news and weather. An air of anticipation seemed to hang over the crowd,

Then, as if on cue, there was a movement toward a hallway. George came over, took me by the elbow and pressed me forward with the others. He was wearing that pleased smile of his, looking like a fat pig. I had been uptight before, but now I was petrified. But for his pressure on my arm I would have turned tail and run.

We descended some stairs at the end of the hall, crossed a semi-dark basement and entered a doorway set in the opposite wall. The door was of heavy metal, as sturdy as a fire door, and I heard, and then saw as I turned, that it was being closed and bolted behind us.

Chapter 6

Any change of heart, any decision to retreat, to call off this insane participation, was now denied me. Go through it I must, see what happens, and express my disgust only at the end.

The room we entered was rectangular, perhaps forty by a hundred feet in size, lit by torches down each side. At the far end a red curtain, closed, extended from wall to wall. We seated ourselves on benches arranged in a semicircle in front of the curtain.

All during our descent into this abyss, as I thought of it, Weston had kept up a running patter with me and others around him, babbling of inconsequential things, his face wreathed in that fatuous smile. Was he but a minor figure in this organization, and was his chatter merely an attempt to flatter his own ego?

A bell rang. The gathering quieted down, facing the curtain. It was drawn back to reveal a half-darkened sanctuary. There was an altar in the center, about waist high, lit by candelabra at each end. Behind the altar a priest stood, robed in black monkish garb, tall, with clean-shaven head, facing the audience. Acolytes, similarly attired, flanked him on either side. Behind and above them, as if suspended in air, hung the head of some grotesque creature, superimposed on an inverted pentagram.

It took only a moment to gather in all of these details. Weston had lied. I recognized the entire scene. A Black Mass was about to be offered here. Weston's organization was no different from any of the others I'd heard about.

The priest raised his arms and began an invocation to the devil, calling upon him with a litany of names beginning with that which Weston had used, AAI, asking him to appear and sanction this gathering. Of course no one appeared. Only the most naïve would have expected it.

I have to admit that I was mentally and physically aroused by all of this, the red and black accoutrements, the flickering candles, the lordly priest, and his acolytes. There were enough sights, sounds, and smells to whet the most jaded and dispassionate appetites. What I was seeing was obscene, even sacrilegious. I knew that. My mind told me to get up and leave, but I could not. I could not had I even dared to make a break for the door and try to unbolt it.

Go along with it, I told myself, hoping to ease my conscience. See what happens. You don't have to be a part of it.

What followed next I must narrate in detail since from it the cult derived its power and inspiration. The doors opened behind us, and a young initiate was led into the hall. The sight was enough to start the pulses racing. She was clad in a long coarse gown, tied at the waist with knotted rope. On her shoulders she carried a wooden beam about five feet long and four inches square. Her arms were bound to the log at the wrists with heavy chains. As she moved—a grotesque parody of the tortured Christ—she stumbled continuously under the load and had to be assisted to her feet by black-robed figures at her sides. Eventually she reached the priest and stood with her back turned to us.

I dreaded the events that were about to take place.

The woman stood facing the altar, struggling to maintain herself under the weight of her burden. The priest stepped forward with his two assistants and addressed her.

"Alaine Marie Ostrano," he intoned, "you appear before me now in this gathering of worshippers, in the sight of AAI, the Lord of the universe, the Prince of the Dark and Holy Places. Let your eyes be open. Set your sights upon the pinnacle of truth, which shall make you free. Seal not your lips, but let your voice be heard aloud as you proclaim your desire.

"Do you, Alaine Marie Ostrano, of your own free and lasting desire, accept this union with all who congregate here, your brothers and sisters, true worshippers of the Ruler of hell and earth?"

There was momentary silence. Then, shakily, "I desire."

"And do you, Alaine Marie Ostrano, accept this, the rebirth of your soul and body, in pain and pleasure, in agony and joy, in wonder and fulfillment, in such measure as may be meted out to you?"

Again, uneasily, "I desire."

"Then, Alaine Marie Ostrano, I bid you welcome. And I urge you to hold fast to that desire which you have proclaimed.

"Let the gates of hell be opened! Receive this woman, thy willing servant, into thy bosom, O Lord AAI, and execute thy judgment.

"Alaine Marie Ostrano! Eliano os operanti!"

These last words were almost shouted. There came a resounding echo from the congregation, which rose to its feet with upheld arms.

A great bustle of activity began behind the priest. Amid a great clanging of bells several black-robed figures appeared and removed the altar. In its place they rolled into the sanctuary a hideous platform roughly eight feet square. At opposite sides were two upright poles with transfixed arms. Near each corner was placed a low brazier.

With the bells still ringing their infernal din the initiate was assisted onto the platform and made to stand facing the congregation. Her face was whitish, frightened. Whatever had been her choice minutes before, only grim determination allowed her to continue.

An acolyte entered the sanctuary bearing a small silver goblet. The priest accepted it, held it aloft, and uttered some further incantations.

"O, thou Lord of the Unseen Darkness, let the dripping of this nectar be sweet to the taste of thy servant, Alaine Marie Ostrano. Let its pollen sanctify the desires of her body and preserve it for thy service.

"With thee, O Great Lord, all things are possible. With thee there is life in death, and life after death. Give this woman strength and courage. Open to her the mysteries of thy creation."

He put the goblet to the woman's lips. She tasted it, found it unpleasant, and turned her head aside. The priest prodded her, however, and she drained the contents.

The priest returned the chalice to the acolyte, turned to face the gathering, and with upraised hands repeated the words he had intoned earlier, "Eliano os operanti!"

Then he stepped aside to allow the unholy scene to continue. There sounded the groaning of a windlass and the clanking of metal as two chains were lowered above the platform. The chains were attached to the beam supported on the girl's shoulders. Now the windlass turned again. The beam was raised slowly, agonizingly, and finally placed on the opposing crossbars at the ends of the platform. The woman hung suspended by the wrists, facing the congregation, her feet barely touching the floor. Chains were next attached to her ankles, securing them to the platform.

Again the priest stood before the woman and with upraised arms repeated his obscene invocation, "Eliano os operanti!"

An acolyte untied the rope about the girl's waist.

"Alaine Marie Ostrano! This is the day of your beginning. This day you shall be born unto life everlasting.

"Come all ye spirits of fire and thunder! Gather now, ye ministers of evil! Here is your victim! Behold! The loins are open! Behold! They await thy pleasure!

"Begin!"

The braziers at the corners of the platform were set afire, the bells began again their deafening ringing, while the priest shook his hands in wild supplication.

I sat riveted to my seat, utterly absorbed in that mad scene. Could I leave? It would have been futile to try. There would have been no escape. Did I want to leave? At the time, no. Later, with that horrible event etched in my memory, I knew that I should have made some protest, some attempt to leave, particularly in light of what followed.

Hooded figures approached the victim, each carrying a knotted rope. The first blow fell across her stomach, leaving a fiery trail. Before her moan had died away a second blow descended upon her back. She jerked in agony, the chains cutting into her wrists and ankles.

Blow followed blow. Welts crisscrossed the trembling body. Blood began to flow.

The congregation sat totally absorbed, I along with them. Criminal? Bestial? Of course it was. And I was as guilty as any of them. Did I make any attempt to stop it? Did I want to stop it? I don't know if I did. There was a fascination, a complete absorption in that insane scene. It was almost as if I were the torturers striking the blows, as if I were the victim receiving them. The engrossment was total and ecstatic.

The beating continued. The screams died away, the body hung limp, the eyes glazed over and closed. And still the torment went on.

The end at last. With a loud cry the priest approached the platform. The torturers moved aside.

He examined the victim carefully, searching for a pulse or heart beat. Apparently there was none. He turned toward the gathering.

"It is finished!"

The body was removed from the cross with much care and wrapped in a white cloth. Hurriedly the platform was rolled offstage and the altar returned. The inert victim was laid upon it.

Now for the first time I moved. I took in a deep breath, let it out slowly and heavily, and made as if to rise.

"No, no!" Weston whispered. "It's not over yet."

Others of the congregation had shifted also, relaxing tensed muscles and nerves. However, no one made any move to leave. All sat hunched forward as if waiting some further enactment.

The priest went over to the altar, his back to us, his arms raised in supplication.

"O, thou Blessed of all Creation, AAI, Lord of Truth and Mercy, in faith and perseverance this woman, thy handmaid, has come to thee, trusting in thy greatness.

"All power is thine, O Lord AAI. Indulge us, we pray thee. In love and gratitude we serve thee."

There was more. How long the priest continued this ungodly harangue I do not remember. What it meant, what he hoped to accomplish, what was to happen, I had no idea whatever.

Which made the ending all the more astonishing. The victim moved. She returned to life. Had she been dead? I had assumed she was. Perhaps she had only lost consciousness. Even so, the recovery was unbelievable. She sat up slowly, shakily, the priest stepping aside so all could see. The scars of her ordeal fell away like molting scales, the flesh reborn before our eyes. In minutes, unbelievably, Alaine Marie Ostrano had been resurrected. She swung her feet to the floor, wrapping the cloth about her in unfeigned modesty. A beatific smile wreathed her features as she stood facing us, extending her right arm to us, the palm upturned and open.

Even from where I sat, even as my mind rejected all that I was seeing, I could discern the black, egg-shaped object she was presenting.

Chapter 7

"So you see," Weston was saying as we drove back, "we are not sadists. We are not pleasure seekers indulging in some medieval debaucheries."

I had not said a word since we left that foul gathering. I felt like some hellish ghoul returning to his resting place after a night of orgiastic merry-making.

"We are legitimate," Weston went on relentlessly, "and we are strong. We are getting stronger all the time."

The first blood-red streaks of morning appeared on the horizon. Memories of the night's ordeal were being etched in my mind.

"But the pain . . . the suffering . . . !" I blurted out at last. "How can you do those things?"

"It is through pain and death that we are born again. Didn't your Christ show you that? The pain is but a moment. The joy, the exuberance is forever!"

"For God's sake, George, don't compare your religion with mine. We don't do those things!"

"How many of your martyrs willingly underwent death by torment? How many of your saints mortified their flesh to better their chance for heaven?"

I could only shake my head. Weston had an answer for everything.

"I wish you would consider what you saw tonight, John. I mean, really put it in proper perspective. You saw a woman die. You saw her brought back to life. This was no trick. This was no magician's stunt. Can your priests do that? How many miracles have your priests performed lately?"

No answer.

"Join us," Weston pleaded. "Believe me, ours is a better life."

"Now wait a minute, George. Are you telling me that everyone who joins your organization goes through this . . . this ritual?"

"Of course."

"Everyone?" I repeated. "You too, George?"

"That's right."

"Do you mean to tell me that you died, as you call it, and came back to life?"

Weston was nodding his head.

"And you went to . . . to hell, or wherever, and came back with this fire?"

"True."

"Aw, George, you expect me to believe that? Well, if you did, tell me about hell. Where is it? What is it?"

"Unfortunately, I can't do that."

"Oh, sure," I sneered, "it's some deep dark secret. You'll let me in on it if I join."

"No, not at all. You see, we have no recollection of what goes on while we are dead."

His jaw set grimly as he said this, indicating that his statement was sincere and that he wished it could be otherwise.

Finally, we came in silence to George's home. I could not wait to get into my own car. I had had enough of Satanism for one night.

I could not brush aside George's pleading, however.

"Think about it, John. That's all I ask. Just think about it. You'll see it our way."

As a parting shot he gave me a copy of his Bible.

"Read it," Weston urged. "It'll explain a lot of things."

I promised to read it, but I lied. I was sure I wouldn't touch that book for anything. I threw it on the seat beside me and drove off. My one thought was to get home, take a long hot shower, and wash away every memory of this hideous night.

During the next few days I lived in a kind of aftershock, torn between remembering and trying to forget. The sensuality of the ritual had fascinated me, I had to admit. But the horror of it, the criminality of it, sickened me in a way I would not soon forget. Join Weston and his unscrupulous mob? Not in a hundred years could I imagine myself doing that.

I did not see Weston for several weeks. He did not report for work. We all came to believe that he had quit. I need not add that few, if any, of us regretted that. One evening, when my thoughts had begun to clear, and memory of that accursed night had retired somewhat into my subconscious, I picked up Weston's Bible out of idle curiosity. There could be no harm in looking at it, could there?

I did not read much.

It began:

> There was no beginning; there will be no end.
> I am always and forever.
> Ages before ages, in the time before time began, I am.
> No woman's womb conceived me; no hand fashioned me.
> I am of the gods; I am God.
> Learn of me:
> I am all and everything;
> I am good and evil;
> I am pain and pleasure;
> I am desire and fulfillment.
> All truth is mine; all power is mine.
> Who shall stand against me, him will I crush forever.

It continued on for several hundred pages. Like some unholy revelation. Like some perverse parody of the Bible.

"Hogwash!" I snorted.

If I had had a fire I would have burned it. Instead I tossed it into my wastebasket.

"You're sick, Weston!" I exploded. "You and your entire, organization. Call up your damned devil, whoever he is, and let him drag you down to hell!"

Chapter 8

Initiations, torture, demonology, heresy, all of these were reason enough for me to shun Weston and his cult. What sabbaths, what depravities were practiced when no visitors were present I dared not imagine.

About a week after this, matters came to a head. On a Thursday evening, I recall, I had been watching television in my apartment, had become bored, and had looked about for something to cure my restlessness. I had tried to put Joanne Weston out of my mind. I hadn't succeeded too well, but I had resigned myself to the inevitable. That part of my life was finished before it ever started.

Suddenly something hit me like a blow to the head. It wasn't anything physical. It was something inside of me, like a thought that jolted me, or . . . or . . . I really didn't know what it was.

For a moment I was stunned. I think I staggered to my feet and tried to get a grip on something. Then I felt another. Like a stab inside my head. Sharp. Painful.

I lurched toward the nearest chair and dropped into it. What was going on? Was I having a stroke? Some brain damage perhaps?

I sat back and tried to relax.

One more such attack, I thought, and, if I survived, I'd call the nearest doctor or hospital.

I was afraid to move, afraid to think. Anything might trigger another attack.

Nothing happened. Twenty, thirty minutes went by. I almost believed I had imagined everything.

Thoughts came into my head. Words took shape. I could almost see them.

"John, join us! John, join us!"

What?

"John, join us!"

I jumped to my feet.

"Weston!" I almost shouted. "Is that you?"

"John, join us!" Over and over.

"Damn you, Weston! Leave me alone!"

"John, join us!"

I bent over in agony. How much of this could I take?

Then there was relief. Suddenly or gradually, I don't remember which. The pain was gone; the voice was gone. For good? Or was it a lull before another attack?

More time went by. Fifteen minutes, thirty minutes. The telephone rang, and I jumped.

I reached for it. "Hello!" I shouted.

"Mr. Pettit?" It was a feminine voice.

"Yes."

"Mr. John Pettit?"

"That's right."

"This is Joanne Weston."

Silence. Shock was following shock.

"Mr. Pettit, can you hear me?"

I got hold of myself. "Oh! Oh, yes, I'm sorry. I can hear you. How are you?"

"All right. I . . . I found your name and number here by the phone on my father's desk . . . and I wondered . . . was he trying to reach you?"

"Reach me?" I played for time. I knew girls were more forward these days, but I didn't feel this was a social call. There was something in the tone of her voice, urgency or anxiety. "Do you think he was trying to reach me?"

"Mister Pettit!" Suddenly she dropped all hesitancy. "Something has happened to my father! I found him lying on the floor here in his den. Are you a doctor? I can't wake him. He's unconscious."

"He's fainted?" Ridiculous question! What I meant to ask was, "Is he dead? Was it a stroke or something?"

"I don't know what to do!" She was verging on the hysterical now. "I was going to call a doctor. Then I saw your name and number. I thought he was trying to reach you."

Lightning finally struck me. This was the chance I had been waiting for! But did I want to take it?

"I'll be there! An hour, maybe less!"

"An hour?"

"It's quite a ways. No, I'm not a doctor. You'd better call one. I'll be there!" I added hurriedly.

"All right." She sounded relieved.

"Cover him. Keep him warm." What did I know about first aid?

I made tracks out of there. Speed limit or no, I wasn't going to waste this opportunity. Fifty minutes later I was at her door.

She looked better than I had remembered. Prettier. Happier.

"He's better." She was smiling now. "He's upstairs in bed."

"Oh. You mean he . . . ?"

"He just fainted," she was hurrying to explain. "He said he'd been working too hard, trying to do too much."

I'll bet he was! Straining himself, that was what he was doing, trying to reach me with his telepathic powers or whatever he was using.

"Do you want to see him?" She asked.

I didn't. "Maybe we'd better let him rest."

She didn't push it.

So now we stood, alone together for the first time.

I groped for words. "How are you?" I asked.

"All right. Fine."

"Did you call a doctor for him?"

"No, he wouldn't let me. He said he was all right."

"He's not working anymore?"

"No, he decided to retire."

"Retire? I didn't think he was old enough."

She laughed. "Oh, he's not that old! I don't mean he retired completely. He's working for . . . for . . ."

"For that organization of his?"

"Yes."

"He's pretty mixed up in that, isn't he?"

"Yes, he is. Are . . . um . . . are you a member?"

"Me? No, I'm not a member."

"But I thought . . ." Her face clouded over. "When you came to dinner, I thought . . . When I found your phone number, I thought . . ."

"You thought I was a member? No, he wanted me to join. I don't intend to."

"Then you don't believe in . . . ?"

"That cult of his? I could never go for that."

"I couldn't either!"

There it was, out at last, the disgust, the loathing she had tried to hide on my first visit. She had been attracted to me, I was sure. I had sensed it, but . . .

We talked for hours while Weston lay upstairs recovering from his experience. That it was he who had been trying to mesmerize me through some hellish power I no longer doubted. But he had given me his best shot and I had survived. Now I had further incentive to resist him—Joanne. She hadn't surrendered either. Years of living with him and she hadn't succumbed.

As it turned out, she knew less about his organization than I did. She had never been to a meeting. She knew only that he was mixed up in something horrid and she wanted no part in it. She had sensed evil in this house and she had taken to wearing a crucifix to protect herself. There were protests from her father of course. She had ignored them.

He wasn't bad, she argued. He had always treated her well. He had just taken a wrong turn somewhere. The lingering, painful death of his wife, he had taken that pretty hard.

I knew better. George Weston was evil. His entire organization was evil. Joanne Weston needed to get out of that house.

She had considered that, she said, but where could she go? She had no close relatives. She had no money. She needed to finish her schooling. So she had hung on, hoping for the best.

Before I left that night I think we both committed ourselves silently to a resistance against Satanism. How we would do this, I didn't know. But we had to try. Someone had to try.

During the next few weeks I saw a lot of Joanne. The attraction that had begun with so much doubt and suspicion now exploded almost beyond control. We held long conversations by phone. We met as often as we dared, secretly, guiltily, afraid that her father did not approve and would separate us at any cost.

Does the path of true love ever run smoothly? We were both novices at the game and we would have to find the answer together, come what may.

Chapter 9

So we met and loved, and loved and parted, and every day was an eternity until we met again. Every pleasant moment was tempered with doubt that we could make our relationship last.

Our suspicions were well founded. George Weston did not approve. He had written me off as a member of his organization without any further discussions on his part or mine. My covert trips to his house to see Joanne, our not-so-secret (I was sure) meetings elsewhere were an aggravation he would not long endure. How ruthless he could be I was soon to learn.

By mid-June Joanne and I had such need for each other that our talks always revolved around the prospects of our living together. Would Weston agree to our marriage? Was it economically feasible on my wages alone? Did we dare share an apartment together, as couples do today, straitlaced as we both were?

Another development seemed to be forcing the issue. Lately Joanne had become so tense and dejected that I began to worry about her health. Living with a father she had come to fear, despising his involvement with cultists, going to various lengths to conceal our relationship—all had brought on a state of nerves that could not be ignored. She had to get out of that house. Soon.

Matters suddenly came to a head.

One afternoon at work I received a tearful, frenzied call from Joanne, asking me to pick her up near her home. It was a matter of more than an hour to find her and bring her to my apartment. On the way back I heard her story. She'd had a heated argument with her father. He was determined to break up our relationship and threatened dire consequences if she continued to see me. She had packed a few essentials and at the first opportunity slipped out of the house and called me.

So now the bridge had been crossed. There appeared to be no turning back.

I will say that the next few weeks were some of the happiest of my life, in spite of the threat we knew to be hanging over our heads. Together, we felt that we could face anything. Nothing mattered. Apart, while I was away at work, for instance, and we were alone with our thoughts, the consequence of our action preyed heavily on our minds. Weston had threatened reprisals. Involved as he was with demonic powers, this could take any form.

Again, the turn of events came quickly. On a Wednesday afternoon, about four weeks after Joanne had moved in with me, I arrived home from work with a sense of great foreboding. The mood had been upon me for most of the day. I had made several attempts to call her and had gotten no answer. She was shopping, I reasoned, but that explanation failed to satisfy me. Now, as I entered the apartment and searched the silent rooms, my worst fears were realized. I hadn't the slightest doubt that Weston had taken matters in his own hands.

"I'll find her, Weston!" I roared. "You can bet on that! And I'll get you! I'll get you if it's the last thing I do!"

In the fastest time ever I arrived at Weston's home.

I rang the bell.

No answer.

I beat on the door.

Still no answer.

"You're here!" I muttered through clenched teeth. "You sure as hell are here. And you're waiting for me!"

Five minutes more of pounding. The door opened.

Weston stood in the doorway, masking his hatred in a look of innocence and surprise.

"John! hello!"

"Where is she?" I demanded.

"Where is . . . Are you looking for Joanne? You mean she deserted you, too?"

"Don't hand me that! You know why I'm here! Where did you take her?"

"My dear boy, I didn't take her anywhere. Come in. See for yourself. You're welcome to search the house top to bottom."

Of course he hadn't brought her here. I had been reasonably certain of that. But I needed to start somewhere.

"Come in, come in," Weston insisted. "You're all upset."

I decided to accept his invitation. I couldn't go running off willy-nilly with no place to look. A conversation with him could bring out some clues, maybe even resolve the situation.

Weston was all solicitude. "Here, sit down and cool off. Let me mix you a drink."

"I don't want a drink. I want to know what you did with Joanne."

"John, John, must I keep repeating this? Joanne is her own boss. She comes and goes as she pleases."

"Hogwash! Joanne is a frightened girl. She came to me because you threatened her, because you drove her out."

For an instant the mask slipped. A flicker of annoyance crossed his face.

"John, I'm going to level with you. I liked you. I took you into my home, I entertained you, I introduced you to my daughter. I offered you the chance of a lifetime with our organization. What did you do? You turned on me. You poisoned my daughter against me. My own daughter! She was the pride of my life. I had high hopes for her. She was to be the high priestess of our cult. But no, you weren't satisfied! You had to destroy everything!"

"High priestess of your cult!" I sneered. "You think she would have joined your crazy organization? She hated every part of it!"

"We have ways, boy. We have ways."

"I'll bet you have!" I retorted. "Initiations, torture!"

"Don't push me, boy."

"Where is she?"

"Where you'll never find her!"

No more pretense now. Now it was out in the open.

I moved toward him, eyes ablaze. "Damn you, Weston, you lying . . . !"

Thraaack!

I staggered backward as if struck by lightning. A bolt of something, sheer energy perhaps, had hit me in the forehead.

"That's just a sample." Weston was saying. "Your kind has to be destroyed, boy. You're dangerous. You and all your kind. We can't let you stand in our way."

Then another flash.

I lost consciousness before I ever felt the pain.

I couldn't move. That was apparent even as I strove to come back to reality. It was almost as if the thought had been implanted in me while I slept: Don't move. You can't.

When my eyes did open, when my dulled senses finally awakened, the reason for my immobility dawned on me. I could have wished that I had remained unconscious.

There was the same scene I had witnessed months earlier, the torch-lit hall, the silent congregation on their circle of benches, the red draperies opened wide, the high priest and his acolytes, the braziers.

But no initiate hung suspended on the dais. Now it was I who hung there. For whatever reason. Who was I kidding? For one reason.

"This one," the priest was saying, "O Prince of the heavenly Darkness, thy servant, John Pettit, who hitherto rejected thee, judge him not, we beseech thee, but let him come to know thee as we know thee, true Lord of the Universe."

There was more, intoned over and over, the same utter nonsense.

Until finally, looking up and seeing me awake, "And so we ask you, John Pettit, in the face of this congregation gathered here before you, to cast aside your denials of the past. Join us now in the ministry of the Lord AAI and all his powers. Speak, John Pettit."

I looked past the priest out into the audience. Was Weston present? He had to be. But the faces turned toward me were many and too dim to be recognizable.

"Do you, John Pettit, accept the rebirth of your soul and body, in pain and pleasure, in joy and agony, in wonder and fulfillment, in such measure as may be deemed necessary?"

Pain? Agony? How long had I been hanging there? My arms seemed to be pulling out of their sockets.

"Weston!" I shouted. "Are you out there?"

That outburst made my chest ache.

"Speak, John Pettit," the priest urged. "Make your wishes known to these, thy friends."

"I hate you!" I shouted.

This was not the answer that was expected. Or wanted.

"Damn you and your whole organization!"

The priest threw up his hands angrily. "Need we question further?"

"Your kind belong in hell, Weston!"

I knew what to expect if I persisted, but did it matter? I was dead either way.

The first blow fell across my back, a complete surprise, and knocked the breath clear out of me. My eyes closed with the sheer agony of it. The next blow almost broke my ribs. I could have doubled up in pain. I almost shouted. I think I cried a little. How much could I take before I cracked completely?

I waited for the next blow. And waited. When it didn't come immediately . . .

"We'll beat you, Weston!" I shouted. "You think you've won? We'll beat you!"

Whrrrp! This time across my stomach.

"I'll come back, Weston!"

Another. And another.

"We'll fight you, Weston!"

Thraaack!

"We'll fight . . ."

Explosions in my chest.

". . . fight . . . and win!"

Thrrrrip!

"Win, Weston!"

Whrrrp!

"Win!"

Whhrrrrupppp!

"I hate . . . you . . . Weston!"

Whhuuurrrruuuppp!

"Hate . . . you . . . Weston . . . hate . . ."

They were the last words I uttered before darkness closed in.

Part Two

Chapter 10

"In here," Weston said, leading me into his library. It was here he had first broached the idea of my joining his cult and introduced me to the stone from hell. A similar stone now rested in my coat pocket. The room had been empty before. Now a dark-haired girl interrupted her typing to look over her shoulder. She seemed vaguely familiar.

"Alaine," said Weston, introducing me, "this is John Pettit. John, you remember Alaine, don't you?"

It was coming back to me, the basement hall, the ritual, the initiate.

"Oh," I answered. "Oh, yes, Alaine . . . um, Alaine . . . um?"

"Ostrano," Weston concluded.

"Ostrano. That's right. I remember now. Sure. How are you, Alaine?"

"Fine," she said.

We shook hands. Dark eyes flashed back at me. Up close Alaine was a very attractive girl.

"John will be working with us for a while," Weston told her. "You two will be working together. I'm sure you'll get along fine."

"My pleasure," I agreed. Could I have imagined a more pleasing situation?

"All right," Alaine agreed. The look she gave me suggested that this arrangement would be equally satisfactory for her.

"As you know, John," Weston continued, "I do research. Religions mostly. All religions, especially Christianity. That's our first target. Once we destroy Christianity, once we show the falsehood of that doctrine, we attack the others. They will simply fall into place."

"I believe you mentioned that once before," I said.

Weston gave me a scrutinous look. "Did I? Yes, I think I did. You remember that, do you, John?"

I nodded. There wasn't much else I remembered about that night, only the room, our conversation about the cult, AAI, and the living flame from hell.

"Good for you, John. Evidently what we discussed sank in. So, as I was saying, this is our research room. That will be your job now, John. It will free me for other things. Alaine will do the typing for you. We have a weekly paper to put out and soon we'll be publishing our magazine. We're growing, John. Before long we'll be nationwide, then the entire continent, other continents. We'll be worldwide. We can do as we please, say what we please.

"You were wise to join us, John. You won't regret it. Christianity is through. It's false, it's stifling. Man wants to be free, to enjoy his brief life on earth. No more of these namby-pamby rules—Don't do this! Don't do that! Who was Christ to tell us what to do? Who is the pope to make laws for us? This is the new age. Society is free, today's lifestyles are free. Who wants to be tied to archaic customs, old traditions?"

I heard him out in silence. When Weston started on this subject it was best to let him have his say.

"So here, John, take off your coat. Sit down. Let me get you started."

I did as he suggested, seating myself at his desk. He pushed some papers aside and presented me with a book, THE book, the New Testament.

"What I want you to do, John, is to browse through this book. Take your time. I don't know how familiar you are with it. Read it, read it as if you are seeing it for the first time. Be open-minded. We're looking for lies, falsehoods, misconceptions, anything."

I was nodding in agreement, but was confused. "Like what?" I asked. "Just what are we looking for?"

Weston took the book from me. "Here, let me show you." He began flipping the pages. "Let's see . . . somewhere about here . . . yes, here we are. You remember the night of the Last Supper when Christ went with his apostles to Gethsemane?"

Weston was reading now. "'He took with him Peter and the two sons of Zebedee and he began to be saddened and exceedingly troubled. Then he said to them, Wait here and watch with me. And going forward a little, he fell prostrate and prayed, saying, Father . . .' and so and so on. 'Then he came to the disciples and found them sleeping. And he said to Peter, Could you not watch one hour with me?'"

Weston looked down at me. "Now, I ask you, John, if the disciples were sleeping, how could they know what Christ was doing? How did they know that Christ wept and 'his sweat became as tears of blood,' as Luke says. You tell me, John."

I couldn't, of course. I had heard that story many times, but had never given it much thought.

"Well," I suggested, "I guess the explanation is, it was revealed to Luke. The Bible is a book of revelation, isn't it?"

Weston waved a hand deprecatingly. "Sure, sure, more divine revelation, right? If you can't explain something in the Bible, just pass it off as divine revelation. That's the easy way out. Here's another for you. This is in Matthew, chapter four. You remember the time Christ was led into the desert by the Holy Spirit and the devil tempted him? Matthew says the devil offered Christ all manner of goodies if Christ would fall down and adore him. So here we have Christ going off alone again, and Matthew is telling us all about it, as if he were there seeing it all. Did Christ tell Matthew? Did the devil tell Matthew? Or is this more divine revelation?"

Weston could not keep the contempt out of his voice. As for me, I had no answer. I seemed to recall that I had challenged him in the past, but I was not too clear about that.

"You see what the Bible is, John? Falsehoods, lies. There's no truth in it. It's a story, make-believe, invention. We're showing it up for what it is."

"Well," I said grudgingly, "I'll see what I can do. I won't promise anything, George. You're a lot better qualified than I am."

"Give it a chance, John. That's all I ask. You may surprise yourself. You're a lot more intelligent than you realize."

"If you say so."

Alaine meanwhile had been standing by, a sheet of paper in her hands.

"I have the new copy for page three ready, Mr. Weston, if you want to look at it."

Weston took it and began to read. "Oh, fine, Alaine. Yes, I see you corrected that one paragraph. This is much better. All right, I'll take this and go over it later. So, I'll leave you two alone to get acquainted. I'm sure this will work out. Any questions, John, you ask Alaine. She's a bright girl. Right, Alaine?"

With that he left the room, giving us a slight upturn to the corner of his mouth. There seemed to be a silent exchange between him and Alaine.

"He's a wonderful man, isn't he?" Alaine asked.

"George?" I considered her for a moment. Medium height, dark-complexioned, Spanish heritage showing in every feature, Weston couldn't have looked very hard at her abilities before hiring her. "He's . . . well, George is George."

"You don't like him?" she asked, frowning.

"Oh, I didn't say that. George is one of a kind. You are either with him or against him. He can be very friendly, very charming. On the other hand, if he doesn't like you . . ."

"He's been very good to me."

"Have you been with him long?"

"About a month. I lost my job. Got fired, really. The company I was with, they heard I was involved with . . . well, you know . . ."

"They fired you for that? Don't they know that's illegal? You can't be fired for your religious beliefs. That's against the law."

"Well, I could have fought it. Mr. Weston wanted to, but I said, No, let it go. It would have been an awkward situation going back there to work. So he offered me a place to stay and work and I accepted."

"You do typing and paste-up for him?"

"Yes, that and," she flushed slightly, "a few other things."

I suspected I might know what a few of those other things might be. When did Weston resist a beautiful girl?

"Well, then," I said, "it's off to work we go. I'm glad we'll be together here, Alaine. Any problems or questions, I'll be sure to call on you. That is, when George isn't around. He is around, isn't he?"

"Pretty much. Makes a lot of phone calls, that sort of thing."

"Right. Well, I won't keep you from your typing. Let's see if I can dig up something here."

"Mr. Pettit," she said suddenly, "can I ask you something?"

"Sure. Go ahead."

"Well, sometimes I'm frightened when I think of it. I mean, I'm Catholic . . . that is, I was Catholic, and now, well, now I don't know what I am. What am I, pagan or what?"

"You're a cultist, Alaine, like me. Are you having doubts? Does George know?"

"Oh, no, no! Please don't mention this to him!"

"I won't say anything, but what's the problem?"

"There's no problem. It's just that . . . it scares me sometimes. We're trying to change the world, aren't we? It'll be different, so different. I wonder what kind of world it will be?"

"It'll be a better world, Alaine. A world where you can do whatever you want. No one will say you nay. No rules, no regulations. Isn't that what you want?"

"Oh, yes!" she agreed, but a cloud still lingered over her pretty face. "But if everyone does what they want, will anyone be safe? Will there be any law and order?"

"Don't worry your head about it," I said. It was a head I would have liked resting on my shoulder. "We'll worry about that when the time comes."

She laughed then. "Okay, Mr. Pettit."

"It's John."

Another smile, prettier now than the preceding one. "Oh, yes. John. I'll leave you alone and get back to my . . ."

"And me back to my job," I said.

I took a seat behind her, picked up Weston's Bible and began randomly turning the pages.

It was not an easy transition to make. Flashing eyes and a bright smile looked back at me between rows of dull, black type. My mind flashed back to another time, another place, to a fifteenth-century abbey and a lone, ascetic monk, struggling to resist the temptation of a hellborn seductress.

How well I would focus on the job Weston had set for me only time and temperament would tell.

Chapter 11

So began my first day with George Weston and his organization. It was a good beginning. The pay matched that of the job I had left, the surroundings were pleasant, and my fellow employee was agreeable and easy to look at.

Why then were there some doubts in my mind? I didn't know, but I suspected that the questions Alaine had raised were ones we might all be asking if Weston's world were accomplished.

Most mornings, Alaine greeted me at Weston's door and ushered me in. I began to look forward to these meetings. Every day should begin like this. Days began to pass at a leisurely pace. I could not have imagined a more satisfying situation. There were no reports to fill out, no one looking over my shoulder. If there was any information I needed, Alaine was quick to supply it. And she responded with an eagerness that belied any mere officious concern.

Weston entered the library occasionally. He had typing for Alaine to do, papers to correct and approve. There seemed to be some sort of compatibility between the two, but how deep it was, what it meant, I could not determine. Certainly he seemed more attentive to her than was suitable in an employer-employee relationship.

As for me, I got along with him equally well. He never pressed me to produce, and he brushed aside my apologies when I confessed I had nothing to offer.

"Tut, tut, John. No sweat. No sweat at all. Relax. When you come up with something, we'll take a look at it."

I tried to assure him that he was more qualified than I. I had been religious in my way, had read chapters of the Bible as well as heard the Gospel read at Sunday services, but I always allowed religious authorities to interpret for me.

One day I believed I had found something Weston could use. When Christ predicted, "Destroy this temple and in three days I will build it up again," it has always been assumed that he was predicting his own death and resurrection. No one successfully challenged that supposition. Now I wondered. When someone speaks in parables and riddles, one can find any interpretation. Like the verses of Nostradamus, like the prophecies of the Old Testament.

I brought the matter up to Weston. "How do we know that Christ was referring to his own body?" I asked. "Why was he always so obscure in his teaching? Why not come right out and say, 'If you kill me, in three days I will live again?' Besides, if Christ died on Friday and rose on Sunday morning, he was dead only about forty hours, not the three days he predicted."

Weston looked at me solemnly for a moment. "Yes, well, I'm glad you are taking an interest in this, John. Of course you are right. Christ was a visionary, a dreamer. He spoke in images, in double meanings. 'Follow me,' he said. Follow him where? Why, to some place in the sky, a world among the stars. Nothing here on earth, nothing that would make life more bearable here and now. No, what he offered was nothing. Nothing at all. Only poverty—'Sell all thou hast and give to the poor'—and persecution—'Take up your cross and follow me'—and restraints like, 'Go and sin no more.' That's nonsense, John. Life is real. Mankind is real. We have one life to live. That's here on earth. After that, what? To kneel for an eternity before some throne and sing Hallelujah? What kind of god would deny us the pleasures of life? Why put man on earth if his only intention was to stifle his needs and desires?"

Weston was off again on one of his sermons. I could only sit and hear him out. Alaine stopped her typing to sit enthralled at his words, like some devotee before her master. I felt rather like a schoolboy who had tried to please his teacher and gotten only a pat on the head for his efforts.

So the days passed with little if any contribution on my part. Frankly, I was becoming a little bored with it all. I was no theologian, no pedantic, no fanatic. A daily dose of the Bible might appeal to ministers and nuns, but as for me, it only served to dull an interest that, like any lay person's, was occasional at best. Is it any wonder then that my interest wandered elsewhere? And where else but to my charming companion?

Olive-skinned, with flashing eyes and a ready smile, Alaine was a picture to attract any red-blooded male. As summer came on and the weather grew warmer, she was dressing to fit the season. Decorously of course, but now she appeared regularly in a tank top and shorts or miniskirt. The sight of that trim figure floated before my eyes, blotting out the verses of Matthew and Mark. I was beginning to feel more and more like that fifteenth-century monk, trying to concentrate on his missal while tempted by a succubus.

I had yet to discover if she and Weston were having an affair. Knowing Weston as I did, I found it hard to believe otherwise. Still, the looks she gave me, the pleasantries we exchanged, all suggested more than a passing interest in me. I would have been a dolt not to see the signs or attempt to take advantage. Let Weston object, let him cry foul, let him eat his own words: "Take what life offers! Give in to your feelings, your desires!" By George then, I was determined to test his convictions, even though I felt sure I might suffer.

"Alaine," I said one afternoon when she had been particularly congenial, "care to have dinner with me tonight?"

Chapter 12

I'd love to have dinner with you," Alaine said to me.
"Great. You don't think George will object, do you?"
She flushed a little. "Why would Mr. Weston object?"
"I see the way he looks at you. I thought maybe you and he . . ."
"He doesn't own me."
"No, I'm sure he doesn't."
"I'm an adult, aren't I? I have the right of free choice."
"Of course you do. You won't get any argument from me."
"You think he'll object?" she asked.
I shrugged again. "Maybe he has rules."
"Rules?"
"About fraternization. After all, we are working for him."
"He hasn't bothered about rules before." Now she blushed a great deal. "I mean . . ." she said quickly, "he . . ."
"You don't have to explain," I interrupted. "What you and George do is your business. You're a young woman, Alaine. You have needs and desires."
"And he wants us to give in to them, doesn't he? Isn't that what this religion is about? Freedom, the right to do what we choose?"
"If it isn't, then he's a big fraud, and it's time we found out. "
"I agree, and I'd love to have dinner with you."

"Fine. It's a date then."

And a date it was.

We had dinner, saw a movie, then dropped into a little bar for a few drinks. We sat in a booth, soaking up the atmosphere of the place, the soft music, the dim lights, totally absorbed in each other. When we rode back to Weston's place, Alaine lay curled up on the seat beside me, her head on my shoulder, eyes half-closed. I could have kissed her then, but I didn't. It was enough to have her near, to feel her body close to mine. I drove with my left hand on the wheel, my right arm around her shoulder. Once, when I patted her shoulder . . .

"Mmmm," she murmured.

"What?" I asked.

"Where are we going?" she wondered dreamily.

"Where do you want to go?"

"Anywhere. Nowhere. To the moon."

"I don't think we can get there in an Audi."

"I don't care. I just want to ride on and on and on."

"We have to stop sometime, somewhere."

"Must we? Then wake me when we arrive. I just want to sleep and dream."

"What are you dreaming about, Alaine?"

"I'm dreaming . . . of a place where it's moonlight and warm and the breeze is soft and cool and the air is filled with perfume and the sky has a million stars and . . . Is there such a place, John?"

"It's where we are right now."

"Oh, yes." She settled more closely beside me. "So don't stop, John. Please! Let's ride on and on to the end of the universe."

I patted her arm and drove a little slower, but inevitably we came to Weston's house.

I kissed her then and she stirred.

"Alaine," I whispered.

"Mmmm? What?"

"You're home."

"Home?"

"Weston's."

She opened her eyes briefly and nestled further against my shoulder.

"And I was having such a nice dream."

"Were you dreaming, Alaine? What about?"

Eyes open completely now, she sat up and shook the hair back from her forehead.

"I don't remember. Isn't that always the way? Where do dreams go when we wake up?" She turned to me sheepishly. "Was I sleeping?"

"A little."

"I'm sorry. It must have been the drinks. I guess I wasn't very good company, was I?"

"You were very good company. I had a great time. Did you?"

Her head drifted back on my shoulder. "I had a wonderful time. I don't want it to end. Does it have to end, John?"

"It doesn't have to end," I said, "but it's late. You need to go beddy-bye if you want to be fresh tomorrow. Do you think you can get in without waking George?"

"I'll be quiet. You really think he objects?"

"I'm sure he'll let us know if he does."

"Well, goodnight." She turned to open the door.

"Alaine," I whispered.

"Mmmmm?"

I kissed her then, not once, but over and over, and she fell back into my arms and we got lost among the stars. Minutes later I stood beside the car and watched as she went up to the house. Pushing the door open, Alaine waved goodnight and stepped inside.

That was when I heard the sound of a window slamming shut in the upper story. As I got into my car to drive back to the city, I knew that Weston had given me his answer.

Chapter 13

"So, how are we doing today?" Weston asked as he came into the library that morning. He turned from Alaine to me and back to Alaine. "After your all-night party," he probably wanted to add.

Alaine's voice quavered as she said, "Good morning, sir."

I stared directly at him. He was my employer, but my guardian he was not. Let him declare himself now if he intended to have it out.

"Okay, George," I said. "And you?"

"Couldn't be better." His lips were stretched in a fat, red smile. "So it's time for work, right, Alaine? You're looking lovely this morning. I'll have some correspondence for you to type later. Right now I need a new inset for page four. I'll get that for you.

"John, how are you doing? Come up with anything yet? Care to do a little editorializing? I can always use some new copy."

"As a matter of fact, George, I do have something to discuss."

"Oh?"

Now it was Weston's turn to stare. I'm sure he was wondering what to expect. I decided to let him simmer for a moment.

"I've been thinking about this lately, George."

He was beginning to fidget uneasily. "Sure, John, out with it."

Alaine looked at me apprehensively. Was I going to make a scene?

"You know, George," I began, "there is something that bothers me." I enjoyed seeing him squirm, but I couldn't drag the situation out much longer. "You remember the story of Adam and Eve? You remember how Cain slew Abel and God cursed him and made him wander the earth?"

Alaine seemed to breathe a sigh of relief. As for George, he was all business now.

"Sure, John, I've read that story many times."

"Well, what happened next puzzles me. Cain went and dwelt in the land of Nod. There he married, started a family, and founded a city. What puzzles me, George, is this: Who was this woman Cain married? Where did she come from? How could there be other cities and people if Adam and his family were the only ones on earth?"

"John, those are old questions. They have been raised many times, once in the famous Scopes trial when Clarence Darrow defended the teaching of evolution. You are right to question it. It is one of the early flaws in the Bible. Next to the story of creation, that is. That is totally absurd. No scientific basis at all. Besides, if you want to believe that Adam and Eve were the forerunners of the human race, and if there were no other people on earth at the time, then their sons and daughters had to intermarry to carry on the species. Imagine the effect this inbreeding would have had on the human race."

"So," I said, "There had to be other people at the time. Perhaps God created them right after he created Adam and Eve."

"Isn't that what evolution is about, John? Man did not evolve singly but in various places over the earth."

"And when we talk about cities like Nod, we're not talking about a Babylon or Thebes or . . ."

"Those first cities were merely collections of tents and huts. They were families clinging together until they got too large, until there was disagreement or until sons and daughter left to start families of their own. It was a nice try, John. And while we're on this subject, you needn't question whether dinosaurs were on the Ark. They weren't. They died out sixty million years before man. Hang in there, John. I'm sure you'll come up with something. The errors are there. You'll find them."

"Well, I'll try. George, but I'm not cut out for this type of thing. You're the expert."

"Don't sell yourself short, John. You know what you're doing or I wouldn't have picked you."

The telephone rang and Alaine hastened to answer it.

"Hello. Yes, it is. This is his secretary. Yes, he's here. What? Wait a . . . !" Alaine was frowning. "Don't you want to talk to . . . Hello! Hello?"

George reached for the phone. Alaine held it for a moment before replacing it in the cradle.

"What was that?" George demanded. He was reddening.

"It's about your daughter, Mr. Weston." Alaine seemed to be trembling. Whether it was because of the news she had gotten or in fear of Weston, I couldn't say.

"What about her?" He shot a sidelong glance at me.

"They say she tried to escape, sir. They're trying to contain her."

"Well, why in hell didn't you give me the phone?" he demanded.

Alaine was looking very frightened. "They told me to hang up, sir. They didn't have time to talk."

"Didn't have time! I'll give them some time! Hand me that phone!" He turned to me. "John, will you excuse me for a moment? I have to make a call."

"Sure, George. Your daughter? I didn't know you had a daughter."

"Talk to you later, John. Do you mind? Please?"

"Right, George, I understand." I gave him a puzzled look and left the room.

I left the door open as I walked down the hall. Even if I had closed it I'm sure I would have heard his explosion behind me.

"Dammit, Alaine, watch what you say. Did you have to tell the whole world about it? I have John right where I want him. I can't have him regressing on me. One more slip like that and hell knows what!"

Chapter 14

I didn't see Weston for the remainder of the day. I heard him leave the house, start the engine of his car and roar out of the driveway. That phone call had disturbed him deeply. It had also raised some questions in my mind. There was one place to get the answers.

I found Alaine in the library. She was sitting at her desk, dabbing at her eyes with a tissue. When she saw me, she tried to hide her feelings with a faint smile.

"Are you all right?" I asked.

"I'm okay," she answered.

"He shouldn't have exploded at you like that. No tact at all."

"It's nothing. It's all over."

Is it? I wondered. "What was that about his daughter?" I asked.

She refused to confide in me. "Please, John, don't ask me. I can't tell you."

"Can't or won't?"

"Can't and won't."

"'Why all the secrecy, Alaine? Is she in some kind of trouble?"

It was the obvious explanation. She had attempted to escape. Therefore she was either in jail, probably for engaging in some occult practices, or she was in a mental institution, which might be worse.

Alaine put her hands to her head to block any further questions. "I can't answer, John. Please don't ask me."

"What am I, an outsider?" I protested. "Don't I belong to this organization? Are there some things I'm not supposed to know?"

Alaine was shaking her head to drown out my words.

"Okay," I said, "you don't have to answer that. But tell me this. How old is she, a teenager or what?"

"She's . . ." Alaine was trying to decide if an answer would be permitted, "about my age."

I had been wondering about Weston's family. "What's her name?"

"Joanne."

"Joanne?" Did a light flash in my head? "Did you say 'Joanne?'"

"Yes, Joanne." She looked at me, frowning. "Why, do you know her?"

"No . . . yes . . . I don't know. That name sounds familiar."

"Do you think you met her?"

"I'm not sure. What does she look like?"

"John, I can't tell you. Honestly, I never met her."

She was desperately trying to avoid my questions.

"Well, what's her problem?"

Alaine put both hands to her head. "Stop! Stop! I can't say anymore. I'll get into trouble."

She jumped from her chair and hurried from the room.

I was tempted to follow her, to apologize, but decided against it. Apparently any mention of Joanne Weston was taboo in this house. At least where I was concerned.

Alaine did not return. I hung around the library until four o'clock, unable to interest myself in anything, interested only in Alaine, asking questions in my mind, trying to solve the mystery of the missing daughter. Joanne Weston. That name kept buzzing around in my head. Who was she? Where was she? Did I know her? Did I know of her?

At Weston's front door I paused to call out, "Alaine, I'm leaving. Can you hear me?" There was no answer. "Alaine!" I shouted. Still no answer. I left the house.

It had been a frustrating day. I was in a particularly foul mood. Over all, I was becoming bored with my work, poring over ancient words, reading and re-reading verses I was already familiar with. I had had twelve years of Christian education and a longer period attending religious services. What was I doing anyway? What was I looking for? Misconceptions, lies? In the Bible? In the Word of God? I must have been crazy to accept this job.

Then there was Alaine. She was constantly on my mind. Now we had had our first argument. Well, not an argument really, not even a misunderstanding. I didn't know what to call it. One thing was certain, however. I was not going to let Weston or any of his family destroy our relationship.

Joanne Weston. Here was a puzzle. Who was she? Where was she? What was her connection to me? Why was the very mention of her name forbidden in this house? Especially where I was concerned.

Lastly, there was George. How well did I know him? What was hidden behind that fat, inscrutable smile? Could I ever trust him? How would he react if Alaine and I . . . ?

And what about that remark he had made in the library, the one I was not supposed to hear? "I don't want him regressing on me," he had said. Regressing? To what? Where did I fit in this puzzle? What was in my past to give him concern?

This was too much for me to consider all at once. I drove furiously back to the city, my one thought being to get as far away as possible from this house of mystery.

Chapter 15

It was late the next morning when I arrived at Weston's. I had had a fitful night with periods of dreaming and sleeplessness. Over and over I apologized in my mind to Alaine, telling her how sorry I was for pressuring her, fearful that she was mad at me and never wanted to see me again. Such are the concerns of lovers.

Between thoughts of Alaine, of life with her and a life without her, I wrestled with the problem of Weston and his daughter. What a mystery this was. Could I have some connection with Joanne Weston? I was certain I didn't know her. Was there a part of my past I had forgotten? I wracked my brain for the answer. Nothing made any sense.

Like a man possessed, I showered, dressed, and raced to Weston's place. I had to see Alaine again, make up with her.

The morning was dark and damp. Halfway there, the sky opened. The rain began with a fierce downpour, then settled into a steady drizzle. The weather hardly improved my mood. I had a sense of impending disaster.

Only Alaine's car was in the driveway. I knocked on Weston's door and, when there was no answer, entered the house cautiously. Alaine was standing near the entrance hall. Could she have been expecting me?

"Alaine?" I whispered.

She didn't answer. There was a half-smile on her face, an embarrassed smile really.

"Are you all right?" I asked.

She nodded sheepishly. Some color came into her cheeks.

"C'mere," I said.

She came to me then, quickly, and my arms went around her.

"Oh, John," she murmured, "I was afraid you were mad at me."

"Mad at you, Alaine? Why would I be mad at you?"

"Just hold me close," she begged. "I'm sorry. I acted like a fool."

"No, you didn't. Don't blame yourself. You were just following orders. I understand."

"Hold me, John. Don't ever leave me again."

"Never," I promised.

Later we sat in the library, discussing many things.

"So, George is away." I repeated the answer she had given me earlier.

"Um-hm. He said he had some business to tend to. I think there's a meeting of the cult tonight."

"You mean, one of those initiations?"

"I think so."

"And we weren't invited? I get the feeling sometimes that I'm not really part of this organization."

"You've gone before, haven't you?"

"Twice. The first time when I saw you. The second is a little hazy in my mind. I don't remember going there, but I woke up and there were all of these people staring at me and I was holding this stone in my hand."

I brought it out of my pocket now. It was solid black, an egg-shaped piece of seemingly ordinary rock. I turned it around and around in my hand.

Alaine was frowning. "Do you really think it came from . . . you know . . . ?"

"I've been wondering about that lately. I suspect it's some kind of hologram. They do amazing things with them these days. This isn't stone either," I suggested. "I'll bet it's plastic."

"But it's so real!"

I smiled at her. "Like our love, Alaine?"

"Oh, John!" She reached for me. "Yes, like our love!"

We kissed then, of course, and enjoyed some innocent touching lovers are permitted.

"Having doubts, Alaine?" I asked later.

"Doubts?"

"About George, about this whole crazy business. What are we doing anyway, getting mixed up in this cult, trying to make over the world? It's ridiculous."

"Maybe . . ." she suggested.

"Maybe what?"

"Maybe," she repeated, "you are regressing, like George said."

"Regressing? Is that what George said? You think I'm losing interest?"

"Well . . ."

"If that is regressing, yes, I'm regressing. I think this whole idea is dumb. Devil worship? That's not for me, Alaine. That's unholy, profane. I'm Catholic, you're Catholic. Do you want to give up your religion, your love of God, your hope for heaven? For what? For this devil, this AAI, that George or somebody dreamed up? It's nonsense."

"But George says . . ." Alaine protested weakly.

"George!" I sneered in contempt. "That man is a fool, a fat, obnoxious, dangerous fool. He's going to destroy himself and everyone with him. He's insane. Do you really want to stay with him?"

She reached out a hand to me. "I want to stay with you, John. I want what you want."

A footstep sounded in the hallway. Alaine and I both turned. George was standing at the door of the library. There was hatred in his eyes and it was directed at me.

"You can leave now, John," he ordered through clenched teeth. "You are no longer part of this organization."

Alaine's hands flew to her throat. I stared at him in complete shock over what was transpiring.

"Get out!" he hissed.

So this is how it ends, I thought. This isn't what I wanted to happen. This was George's scene.

I started to explain. "Look, George, I . . ."

"Get out!" he insisted, louder now. His face was turning very red. "You're finished, through, kaput."

"Okay," I said. I was resigned to the inevitable. "I'm going, George." I turned to Alaine. "Are you coming, Alaine?"

"Alaine is staying," he snarled.

Now it was my turn to bristle. "Well, George, I think that's up to her. Isn't that right, Alaine?"

"She has no say in the matter," George demurred. "Neither do you. Now get out before I throw you out."

I wasn't going to let him get away with that. "Careful, George. It'll take a better man than you to throw me out."

"Don't be so damn sure!" George roared. "I took care of you once before. I can do it again."

I had no idea what he meant, but I decided it was best to retreat. I couldn't afford to make a scene in his house.

George followed me to the door, trying to block my view of Alaine.

"Alaine!" I called out. "I'll phone you! I'll get in touch with you."

She was in tears, the pain of parting on her face.

"You come near this house again," George was saying, "you come anywhere near Alaine, and you're dead! You got that?"

"I'd be careful with threats like that, George, if I were you. You're a fraud. Your whole organization is a fraud and I'm going to prove it."

"Go to hell!" Weston roared. He was shoving me toward the door with his stomach, fists clenched at his sides.

The door slammed shut and I was outside. I had a sudden feeling of déjà vu, of having stood at this same door once before and being challenged.

Something was awakening in my mind, a part of me that had gotten lost.

"Damn you, Weston!" I shouted and pounded a fist on the door. "I'll be back! I'll be back for Alaine, and we'll destroy you and your whole damned organization!"

How I would do that, how I would rescue Alaine, I hadn't the slightest idea in the world.

Chapter 16

I was out of a job. Next to my fears for Alaine's safety, alone in that house with a devil worshipper, alone with a man who could be as ruthless as he was charming, my most pressing need was finding employment. I had rent and car payments to make, as well as ordinary living expenses to meet. My wants were few, but the simplest things in life can acquire paramount importance when they are just beyond reach.

There was a chance, I thought, that I could get rehired at Smith and Holmes. We had parted on good terms.

"As a matter of fact," Jim Kimbrough, the department manager, said when I sought him out that afternoon, "I will have an opening in about a week or so. Mary Shaughnessy—you remember her—she's due for some surgery. I don't know just when, so I'll be needing a fill-in. It'll be temporary, John, but then again, maybe not. We'll have to see."

It was as much as I could have hoped for and it solved my immediate need.

That left the problem of Alaine. How was I to get in touch with her? Weston was sure to block every attempt. And if I were successful, what then? Would I bring her back to my apartment? Marry her? I loved her of course, and I was sure she loved me. But I wasn't sure if I was prepared for a lifetime commitment.

I made several calls to Weston's house throughout the afternoon and evening. The phone rang and rang but no one answered. That was to be expected. It was frustrating, nevertheless.

"Damn you, Weston!" I repeated over and over.

How simple life would be without the Westons of this world. History is full of abrasive personalities who complicate our existence, who run roughshod over ordinary people and make their lives a living hell.

"I'll get you, Weston," I vowed. "I'll make you pay, count on that."

Weston had threatened murder if I tried to get in touch with Alaine. Idle threat or not, he undoubtedly meant business and he would take any steps to prevent communication between us. Isolating Alaine was one possibility, but how long could he keep her locked up in her room? Disconnecting the phone or changing the number were other options. Neither appeared to have happened so far, perhaps because the phone company needed time to do the job.

It was likely that Weston would appropriate Alaine's car keys. That would inconvenience her for awhile. Eventually she would escape from the house and get to a phone. There was also a possibility that she was no longer in the house. He could hide her anywhere. I dreaded that prospect. If I never saw her again . . . if, if, so many ifs and no solutions.

I considered another possibility. Weston had a gift of persuasion, and Alaine was young and impressionable. Under the spell of his rhetoric she might even now perceive me to be her enemy, a threat to her future, to her mentor, to the cult. While she had expressed a desire to be with me, to want what I want, she hadn't admitted any desire to leave the organization. When and if I got to her, I might find myself in a situation I was not prepared to handle. Suppose she refused to leave Weston? Suppose she believed her future was with the cult? The wealth, position, and unbridled pleasures it offered could turn anyone's head.

It was late that evening when an idea hit me and wouldn't go away: drive out to Weston's and reconnoiter the place.

It was an absurd idea. It would mean an hour's drive at midnight to go snooping around in the dark when everyone would surely be sleeping. There was a possibility I could be caught trespassing and charged with attempted robbery. And what would I hope to accomplish if I discovered anything—break into the house and try to rescue Alaine? What if she didn't want to leave, or couldn't, and I had to confront Weston? He could be nasty.

Weston lived in a slightly wooded area in an unincorporated part of the county. I pulled off the road a short distance from his place, got out, and started walking. I had never done anything like this in my life. I didn't relish doing it now. I felt like a criminal. At any moment I expected a squad car to pull up beside me. There would be steel in the officer's eyes as he stepped out and suspicion in the questions he asked me, "Sir, may I ask where you are going? Do you have some identification?"

I would have to lie, of course. "Sir, my car broke down. I'm looking for a telephone." It was a suitable answer and he ought to accept that. I only had to remain calm and hope he didn't ask other questions.

I came upon the house rather suddenly. I had to get back behind a tree for fear of being seen. It was unlikely that anyone would be watching, but in my state of mind I was fearful of everything. The house was of colonial design, gray frame with attractive white trim. How could a house so normal looking harbor so much evil? But then, how could a man like Weston, so charming at times, be the personification of that evil?

The house was dark and quiet. Either everyone was asleep or the place was empty. Not deserted perhaps, merely empty for the time being. Weston's car was not in the driveway. Neither was Alaine's. Then I remembered something she had said earlier. There was to be a meeting of the cult this evening. I looked at my watch. The time was slightly after one. If past meetings were any indication, Weston would not be back for another hour. It was all the time I needed to get to Alaine and take her away. Was I willing to risk it?

Alaine's room was on the second floor, but I didn't know where. It seemed likely that it would be in the rear. I decided that would be the logical place to start. I stole from tree to tree, keeping one eye on the house. To say that one's nerves relax somewhat when the body takes action is not entirely correct. I was moving into further danger and I was dying a thousand deaths.

The Cult of AAI

The rear of the house was dark also. There were eight windows at ground level, plus a small porch. Directly above this was a large picture window, flanked by four sets of windows. Behind one pair had to be Alaine's room, but which one?

I tried the door of course. It was locked tight, built of solid wood, and I had no way of opening it. I had come away with nothing, not even a flashlight to guide me if I managed to gain entrance.

I tried calling her name. No answer. Even if awake, it was unlikely she would hear me with all the windows closed. I was afraid to shout. I had to strike a happy medium between getting her attention and calling attention to myself.

I looked for a ladder, pole, tree, anything to reach the upper floor. There was nothing. Then I remembered the trick used so often in movies. I searched for a rock or pebble in the grass. I found a clump of dirt, stood under the left windows and heaved. The dirt disintegrated as I let it fly.

I was losing valuable time. Perhaps forty-five minutes remained. I hadn't found Alaine and I might yet have to do some convincing to get her to leave.

I kept looking for pebbles. It wasn't easy under a cloudy night sky. Then I found something I thought I could use. It was larger than I needed, a piece of used brick, but it was sure to be effective. I took careful aim, gauged the distance, and let it fly.

I thought the crash would wake the entire county. I had to run for cover as the glass disintegrated and a shower of broken shards rained down from above. From behind a tree I stared up at the broken window, hoping for success, yet fearful of the consequences. If Alaine was in that room, she was awake now and frightened. If George had set a trap for me . . .

A white figure appeared at a window. Was it . . . ? It was! Hands placed cautiously against the frames, Alaine peered out, looking for answers.

I ran from my cover. "Alaine!" I yelled. "It's me, John!"

I saw recognition come into her face. "John!" she exclaimed. "Oh, John!" She said it over and over. I had been a fool to doubt her.

"Open the door!" I shouted. "Are you alone?"

"Yes, yes! Oh, I'll be right down!"

I heard her fumbling at the door, saw it swing back.

She flew into my arms and cried. Maybe I cried a little, too, tears of happiness, tears of relief. We clung together for several minutes before I came to my senses.

"Alaine," I whispered. "we've got to get you away. If George finds us . . ."

"I know!" she said. "Oh, John, it's been awful. I thought I was never going to see you again!"

"Me, too. I called and called. Nobody answered."

"He wouldn't let me! He said if I did . . . Oh, John, I was so afraid!"

"No more," I told her. "You don't have to be afraid anymore. Where is he, by the way? At one of those meetings?"

"Yes. Oh, John, if he comes back and finds you . . ."

"So come with me," I pleaded. "Let's go now."

"Really, John? You mean it?"

"I mean it. Pack your things and we'll get out of here."

She kissed me then, and I followed her as she flew up the stairs to her room. Between more kisses she dressed hurriedly and packed two suitcases. Meanwhile I kept one ear tuned for George's return, We left by the back door, stole around the side of the house, and took cover in the trees.

This had been easier than I expected and more successful than I had hoped. I raced back to the city, to my apartment, and there, safe in each other's company, we embraced as only lovers do when they have lost each other and been found.

It was a short time later, as we sat on my couch, happy with our success and secure in each other's company, when a thought struck me and I bolted upright.

"Oh, my God!" I moaned.

A feeling of déjà vu had swept over me. I had been in this situation once before.

"What's the matter?" asked Alaine.

For a moment I was unable to speak. I'm sure I turned white as a sheet. Alaine was staring at me.

"What is it?" she insisted. "What's wrong?"

"I remember," I muttered. "I remember everything now."

"You mean . . . ?"

I nodded and held my head in my hands. Then I let out a groan as I uttered the name neither of us wanted to hear.

"Joanne."

Chapter 17

It had been too easy. I should have known. "The best laid plans . . ." Robert Burns was right. When, if ever, was man master of his fate? The ancients would have cursed the gods for having sport with them. I could only sit and wonder why my life, which had been so lackluster, had, in a few short months, become filled with friction and confusion.

"Joanne?" Alaine repeated, frowning. "Do you know George's daughter?"

What a shocking development this was. I not only knew her, I had rescued her under similar circumstances, and I had brought her here and lived with her.

And I had loved her.

My dismay was spreading to Alaine. There was suspicion in her voice as she asked, "Did you . . . did she . . .?"

I couldn't face her. I looked down at the floor and nodded. I didn't dare answer.

"What happened?" she wanted to know.

How could I tell her? What could I tell her? I remembered it all now, the arguments at work, dinner at Weston's, my meeting with Joanne and her apparent dislike, AAI and the stone from hell, Alaine's initiation into the cult, my horror and rejection,

Joanne again, and a love that grew despite Weston's hatred, sharing this apartment together, then losing her, Weston's revenge and my initiation into the cult.

It was all clear now. I had hated Weston from the start. Somehow the initiation had changed me. Somehow Weston had brainwashed me into joining the cult and had me working for him. The only uncertainty was how he had managed it.

"John, please, I need to know," Alaine was pleading.

I couldn't. Joanne's face floated before me, that sweet, innocent face, so distrusting of her father and all he stood for. What could I say? What was I to do? I couldn't be in love with two women, could I? How could I love one without hurting the other? And in God's name where was Joanne? Where had she attempted to escape from? How could I find her? Did I want to?

Alaine moved as if to disengage herself from me. I had a moment of sheer panic. She was hurt and needed to know the truth. If I didn't open up, I could lose her forever.

"Yes," I said, "I know Joanne. We lived together here at the apartment. That was months ago."

I spilled it all then, and she heard me out with remarkable patience.

"Do you love her?" she asked at last.

"Yes. No! I don't know. I did once. Now, if I ever saw her again . . ."

I grabbed Alaine and held her tight. "Alaine," I begged, "you have to understand. I haven't been myself. Weston . . . that bastard . . . he did something to my mind, blocked out my memory. You see that, don't you? You forgive me?"

I felt her head nodding next to mine and I held her tighter.

"We have to fight him, Alaine. We have to find a way. He'll be coming for you. You can bet on that. What he did to Joanne, I don't know. Whatever it was, I can't let that happen to you. Alaine, I can't lose you, too!"

As we clung together in fear and determination, I knew where my heart lay and what I had to do. Weston was dangerous. He had powers that seemed extraordinary. But this time I was forewarned and with God's help I would see him destroyed.

Chapter 18

I didn't relish going back to work. Nor was Alaine happy to see me go. She feared Weston now and she believed, as I did, that he would attempt to bring her back.

"I'm so afraid," she breathed that first day.

Her fears cheered me to no end. They indicated a complete break with Weston. If I had any doubts about her loyalty, about her love for me, the feelings she expressed now dispelled them completely.

"I know you are," I agreed, "but let's be practical. He's only a man. What can he do? Come here and carry you away by force?"

"But didn't he . . ."

"Joanne was his daughter. Maybe the law was on his side. I don't know. If he comes, scream, yell, kick, fight, call the police, call me. I'm only fifteen minutes away."

That soothed her a bit, and our parting was too sloppily sentimental for me to describe.

A week had passed since she moved in with me. Nothing untoward had occurred, but tension was mounting rather than diminishing. Weston was biding his time. One day he would strike and the same scenario might be written, a repeat performance of my affair with Joanne.

Here was a problem that occupied my mind. A scant six weeks had passed since Joanne and I shared this same apartment under similar circumstances. I felt her presence still. There were moments when I wondered who was in my arms, who did I want in my arms. And there was the constant need to know where she was, how she was, and did she love me still. For a man whose life had been so normal, I was now living in something of a nightmare. How would it end? When would it end?

Saturday came at last. My first week back at Smith and Holmes was over. I looked forward to spending two full days with Alaine.

"Oh, John, let's do something!" she begged. "Let's go where George could never find us!"

Where would that be? I wondered.

"Let's fly down to Rio," I proposed. "We'll climb Sugarloaf Mountain and sip rum under the stars. Or," I said, "we could be practical and . . ."

"Wherever!" said Alaine, and closed my lips with hers.

We settled on an inexpensive dinner and a movie afterward. Back in the apartment we made ourselves comfortable, propped pillows beneath our heads and watched late night television in our bed. There are few moments like this, cozy and safe in one's own retreat, the world a million miles away, our hearts warm with love and togetherness.

Alaine's head was on my shoulder, my arm around her. We were as one in mind and body. When she lifted her head a little, I supposed she was stretching to snuggle closer.

"What . . . ?" she asked softly.

"What what?" I said.

"I thought . . . ?" She was no longer looking at the set. She was peering into a corner.

"What's the matter? Hear something?"

"I thought . . . over there . . . Did you see something?"

She had raised up now and was pointing. I looked. I saw nothing.

"N-no." She relaxed again. "I guess not."

"Jumpy, are we?" I pulled her back to me and nuzzled her neck. "Get back where you belong, you delicious little . . ."

Snap!

We both jumped as if the mattress springs had suddenly been released. The television set went blank and was sputtering amid a shower of sparks and smoke. Alaine huddled closer to me while I tried to remain calm. Tense as we were lately, it hadn't taken much to startle us. Weston was always on our minds. Anything untoward could be attributed to him.

I soon saw the normalcy of the situation. "Damn!" I groaned. "Now we need a new TV set." For Alaine's sake I refrained from adding out loud, "Where do I get the cash for that?"

But she wouldn't have heard me anyway. She was staring into the corner again and pointing.

"John, look! What's that?"

We both saw it then. A bluish-gray mist was growing in the corner. Smoke! I needed to unplug the set.

But Alaine held me back. "John, it's . . . it's . . .!"

In the mist a face was appearing. It was a face we had come to know so well. Weston's! Life-sized, that face was staring at us, a sardonic smile on the lips, speaking words that brought fear to our hearts.

"Did you think you could escape me," Weston sneered, "you miserable beings with your petty little minds? You don't understand, do you? I am AAI! I am the god you worshipped. I can destroy you with one thought as I destroyed your TV. I want you, Alaine, and I will have you. Who will protect you, that pitiful scum of a being beside you? Once before he thought he could foil me. This time I will crush him like a bug underfoot. Enjoy your little tryst, now. Be happy in your neat little nest. I bide my time. I will come and I will be avenged!"

The voice faded along with the sneering face.

Then the light exploded on the wall above our heads and we were left in total darkness. We lay huddled together, fearing his next attack and wondering when it would come. The evening that had begun so happily had turned into a night of terror.

Chapter 19

It was obvious we would not be able to fight Weston alone. He was far too powerful for that. But where could we turn? My first thought was to the police. Would they believe us? Alaine suggested we try the Church. I yielded.

Father Masterson was Irish through and through, one of a long succession of such pastors and assistants at St. Bridget's Church. There wasn't a trace of a brogue in his speech however.

"So, what can I do for you?" he asked as we sat before his desk. An open appointment book and a look of bemused anticipation suggested that he knew why two young people had presented themselves at his rectory. He couldn't have been more surprised and more mistaken.

"Father," I began. I fumbled for words. How do you explain that you believe someone is a devil? How do you convince someone that you are a rational human being and not hallucinating? "We are involved with a man . . . his name is George Weston . . . who has an organization called the Cult of AAI. They practice Satanic rituals and this man Weston seems to have extraordinary powers."

"He is evil," Alaine chimed in, shuddering.

"I know you won't believe this, Father, but this man is after Alaine, and unless we get help somewhere, I'm afraid she isn't going to be safe."

The smile on the priest's face had disappeared. He leaned back in his chair, contemplating us with furrowed brow and pursed lips. It seemed an eternity before he spoke.

"Are you members of this parish?" he asked.

"I am," I said. "Alaine isn't."

"St. Ferdinand's," Alaine admitted.

"I see." Father Masterson glanced down at Alaine's fingers. "You two aren't . . . ?"

"We're not married."

"But we're living together," Alaine added, then immediately blushed as if she wished she hadn't said that.

Father Masterson kept his counsel to himself. "This man, you say his name is . . . ?"

"George Weston."

"And you say he is a devil?"

"He claims to be a devil called AAI. I know this sounds crazy, Father, but if you knew him as we do, if you saw the way he operates . . . He has strange powers. He can control minds."

"One night he came to us in a mist," Alaine said. "He wanted me to come back to him."

It was obvious the priest wasn't believing any of this. We would have to be more convincing.

"Alaine and I were both members of his cult. Well, I was tricked into joining, Alaine wasn't. But we both left. Now he's after her. He threatened me. He knows I hate him and he knows I love Alaine."

"And he has a daughter," Alaine continued. "He hid her and John doesn't know where she is."

Father Masterson drummed a light tattoo on his desk and looked around the room uncomfortably.

"John, that's your name, isn't it?"

I nodded.

He turned to Alaine. "And you are . . . ?"

"Alaine."

"Right. John and Alaine. Well, why are you telling me this? What would you have me do?"

Yes, I thought suddenly, what did I expect him to do?

"Are you suggesting I perform some sort of exorcism?" he asked. "Say a few prayers and make him disappear?"

There was an amused turn to the corners of his mouth.

"We don't do exorcisms anymore. Oh, in rare cases perhaps, when the evidence is substantial. I don't do them, certainly, and I would hate to bring such an idea to my superiors."

"Don't you believe in devils?" asked Alaine incredulously.

"The devil isn't flesh and blood, Alaine. The devil is a spirit. He works within us, tempting us with bad thoughts, bad desires. There may have been instances when the devil appeared in the flesh, once when he tempted Adam and Eve, again when he took Christ up in the mountain. Demonic possession, yes. There are many instances of that. In the Bible certainly. But you are not suggesting demonic possession here, are you? You're claiming this man is a devil, a real flesh-and-blood demon?"

"Well, that's what he claims, and he surely has some strange powers."

Father Masterson was getting up. He was dismissing us.

"Yes, well, John and Alaine, thank you for coming to me with your problem. Unfortunately, I can't help you. I really don't have time to discuss this further. I'm sure you believe what you say. You look like intelligent people. Maybe you should forget this. Perhaps you are overreacting? Seeing things that aren't there? Seeing too many horror movies?"

The disappointment was clear on Alaine's face. How could he not believe us? I withheld any further comment. It would be useless. The priest had already made up his mind.

"You can take comfort in the thought that God is always with us," Father Masterson continued. "He loves us and He watches over us. Sometimes we worry needlessly about things that are never going to happen. We need only to pray for guidance and protection, hmm? Ask His help over the rough spots. Be brave, be prayerful, be hopeful. God knows what is best for us."

There was more, intoned over and over, words he had probably used countless times before.

I led Alaine to the rectory door. We shook hands with Father Masterson.

"Thanks for seeing us," I said.

"Yes, thank you." This from Alaine.

"That's quite all right," the priest answered. "If I can be of any help in the future, well, I'm always here."

The door closed behind us. He was probably shaking his head as he turned away.

"What do we do now?" Alaine asked as we settled in my car. "Talk to the police?"

"The police?" I laughed. "Honey, if the Church doesn't believe in devils you can bet the police won't! No, we're on our own. It's you and me against Weston. But we can beat him. We'll just have to find a way."

Chapter 20

Find a way, I muttered to myself. Easier said than done. Fighting crime, fighting society, fighting governments, mankind has been butting its head against wrong-doers and wrong-thinkers throughout history.

Sometimes successfully.

Fighting supernatural powers? Fighting evil that defies all natural explanation? How were we to do that? It would take powers that exceeded Weston's abilities.

Whose but God's? But we had appealed to Him through His priest and gotten nowhere.

If we must fight Weston, if we were to win over his satanic energies, we might need a miracle. I had to keep this from Alaine. Let that pretty head have full confidence in me. Her confidence would strengthen my resolve.

I believed I had found help two evenings later. Coming back to the apartment after work, I was in high spirits.

"Alaine," I said, "guess what? I think I found someone who can help us."

"Oh? Who is that?" she wanted to know.

"Well, every day I pass a little place called The Alchemist's Shoppe. I always wondered about it, and today I decided to stop and see what it's all about. Alaine, you should see this place! It has all kinds of books on witchcraft and satanism and charms and magic potions. They have stuff to ward off evil spirits and put spells on people. I was talking to the owner and she is into voodoo and black magic. I mentioned George Weston and his cult and she knows about him. She says he is an evil person. I really think those two are at odds with each other."

"Do you think she can help us?" Alaine wondered.

"Well, she said if we will come by this evening or any evening, she'll hear our story and we can go from there. It's worth a shot."

"Fine," said Alaine. "Now give me a kiss like you always do. I miss you all day. Don't you know that?"

It was a strange place with a dank, musky smell, as if it had been culled from a wizard's cellar. The walls were lined with shelves holding bottles and jars, all labeled with exotic names. Most seemed to be in Latin, while others were in a language only a linguistic expert could recognize. The bottles held liquids of every color, from palest tan to bright blue to deep crimson. One could imagine what the latter bottles contained, or purported to, if one was at all skeptical.

Two glass-topped counters ran lengthwise down each side of the store and held other wonders—precious stones of such magnificence we gasped in awe; crystals that seemed to flash of their own light; and insects of many sizes and shapes, neatly pinned to pieces of cardboard or preserved in plastic boxes. Alaine turned from the scorpions and spiders and grimaced.

But we had no time for browsing. The owner was standing there, waiting for us.

"Honey," I said to Alaine, "this is Madame Zangara, the lady I was telling you about."

She was a large, heavy woman, and the flower-print, full length gown she wore did little to lessen that impression. A bright bandana covered her head but left exposed two large rings of gold piercing her ears. The face was middle-aged, the complexion a light tan, the expression open and friendly. My first thought had been that she was mulatto. Now I wasn't sure. Jamaican, African, Hawaiian, did it matter?

"I'm pleased to meet you," Alaine said. She offered her hand.

Madame Zangara gathered her up like a mother bear enveloping her cub. Alaine was smothered in that huge embrace, her face turned aside, her eyes seeking mine, begging for relief.

"But she is charming!" said Madame Zangara. "Isn't she charming?" she asked me. "Your wife is delightful!"

Released, Alaine tried to compose herself. "We're not . . . married," she said, smiling embarrassedly.

"So what does that matter?" asked Madame. She snapped her fingers. "Marriage! Poof! I care that for marriage. It is love that matters. It is love that holds us together."

She grabbed Alaine again and swallowed her as before. "And I see that you are so much in love. The señorita, she is charming." She turned to me. "Is she not charming?"

"I think so!" Would I have said otherwise even if it were not true?

Again Madame Zangara released her and Alaine was uncomfortable as she brushed her hair and smoothed her dress.

"So now we have a problem. Is it not so?" asked Madame. "This Westone, he is an evil man." She snapped her fingers. "Poof! I care this for him!"

We cared little for Weston likewise, for Westone, as the Madame called him, but it would take more than dislike to thwart him. Was Madame up to it?

"We will talk," she said. "But first I will lock the door. No one will interrupt us."

She led us into a back room. It was small and dark, lit by a globe lamp set on a velvet-covered table. We seated ourselves at one side opposite Madame and waited for her to begin.

It took little imagination to realize that this was a private room for secret and mysterious practices. Alaine edged closer to me, very much ill at ease.

Madame Zangara was not at all hesitant. "So now you will tell me all about Westone."

We did. The Madame seemed unconcerned about time, as Father Masterson had been, nor was she the least bit skeptical. We told it all, first my experience with Weston, then Alaine's. She had met him through a mutual friend, had succumbed to his charm—yes, he could be charming at times!—and being impulsive by nature had joined his organization.

"It is as I thought," Madame said when we had finished. "This Westone, he is all bluff and blubber. I care that for him!"

Another snap of the fingers. "It is good you come to me. I will give you charms to protect you. You will see. That Westone, he is an evil man, but he has his weakness. You must not worry. Madame will do all she can."

Chapter 21

I'll say this for Madame Zangara, she exuded confidence. What abilities she possessed and how well she would perform, only time would tell.

"Thank you for seeing us," I said as I led Alaine to the door.

Alaine stayed close, as if she feared another cloying embrace. "Yes, thank you," she murmured.

"We knew we needed help, but we didn't know where to turn," I added.

"How could I not help you?" Madame insisted. "The señorita... ah, but you are both charming. And that Westone, we will fight him, you will see."

Alaine and I slept soundly for the first time in several nights. Madame gave us gold chains to wear around our necks with curiously marked disks attached. Tokens though they were, we felt as if Weston's wrath had been lifted from our heads.

The religion Alaine and I both observed forbade belief in charms, magic potions, black magic, mysticism, all of the occult practices Madame Zangara employed, but where was the harm? Besides, having been involved with satanic rituals the past few weeks, the practices of Madame Zangara seemed tame by comparison.

The Cult of AAI

So we slept peacefully that night and every night that week, and every morning I left for work, confident that Alaine would be safe.

It was the following Sunday when the bomb figuratively exploded. The news appeared in every paper and in every television report.

"Satanic cult raided in county."

"Police halt secret rituals in basement."

"Devil worshippers arrested. Cult disbanded."

Alaine and I read and listened to it all. One can imagine the delight and relief we felt. Was it over? Were we free of Weston? Had Madame Zangara been part of it?

I called to offer congratulations.

"But no," she said. "I take no credit for it. It is God's punishment perhaps. Someone informed the police. In the end, evil will lose. Always. You will see. But I have other news for you. It is not good. You have not heard? This Westone, he is not captured. He is free. Where he is, the police do not know. I do not know. I fear he may be even more dangerous now. We must be careful. Come to me tomorrow evening. We will see what we must do."

Alaine, standing next to me, heard none of this, but she could tell by the expression on my face that something was amiss.

"What is it, John?" she wanted to know. "What's the matter?"

Would it be wise to tell her and worry her needlessly? I felt I must. If we were to see Madame the next evening, Alaine should know everything.

"It's Weston. They didn't get him. Somehow he escaped. They don't know where he is."

"Oh, Holy Mary!" There was consternation in the face she presented to me. "Suppose he comes here! What will we do, John?"

"Now, now, honey," I pleaded. I gathered her to me and held her tight. "Let's not worry too much about this. Why would he come here? He's on the run. He'll get as far away from here as he can."

"Do you really think so? Oh, John, if something were to happen to you, to either of us, I don't know what I'd do!"

"Nothing's going to happen, Alaine. Madame Zangara said she'd protect us, remember? She knows what she's doing. She wants us to see her again tomorrow evening. We'd better go."

"All right," Alaine agreed. "But let's not leave each other for an instant. Promise?"

I promised.

What good are promises that can't be kept? What good are metal charms against the forces of evil? Despite my pledge to Alaine I reported for work the next morning. Alaine was fretful as she said good-bye.

"Must you go?" she asked for the umpteenth time.

"Honey, you know I have to. I need the job and we need the money. What do we live on, love?"

Thankfully, Alaine didn't answer with some romantic cliché of her own.

"Hurry back," she begged. "I'll be worrying all day."

I tried to make light of her fears. "No need to worry. We've got our lucky charms, remember? That ol' black magic? Ooooooooo! I'll be home before you can stuff your peppers and boil your potatoes."

"I'm not stuffing any peppers and I'm not boiling any potatoes. And if you're not home early you may not get any dinner at all."

"Well, I can always eat out . . ."

"Don't you dare!"

I called Alaine at noon. She was safe, but lonely, and still worrying needlessly. I was having a few qualms myself, but I couldn't admit that to her. You can be sure I tested the speed limit on my way back to the apartment. She had taken complete control of my life, my thoughts, my emotions. I longed to see her face light up as I opened the door. I wanted my arms around her and her head on my shoulder. I wanted to enjoy the nearness of her, the fragrance of her skin and hair.

I used my key and pushed open the door.

"Alaine!" I called.

I stepped inside.

"Honey, I'm home."

No answer.

"Alaine, where are you? Can you hear me?"

I had a sudden chill down my spine.

"Alaine!"

I went from room to room. Not in the kitchen, not in the bedroom, not in the shower. She was not in the apartment.

"Weston!" I screamed.

Then I dropped down on the couch and buried my face in my hands.

Chapter 22

"Give it up," a voice within me pleaded. "You can't win. You're in over your head."

Yes, give it up, I reasoned. How could I fight Weston on my own? The man was amazing, Nothing deterred him. In the end he always won.

Which was why I wouldn't give up.

"Damn you, Weston!" I roared. "You think you've won?" My blood boiled as I recalled that fat face and that hellish smile. "I'm coming after you. I'll beat you, count on that!"

Brave words, easy to utter in the heat of the moment. But I would get help. One avenue was still open to me.

"We can't do anything for forty-eight hours," Sergeant Haller advised me that afternoon.

"I know all about that," I said grudgingly. "But that's stupid. In forty-eight hours she could be halfway across the country or out of it."

"I don't make the rules, sir. I follow them."

What do I do now? I wondered. I had been to the Church, to Madame Zangara, and now to the police. Must I work alone?

"We are making every effort to locate this Weston. He is holed up somewhere, so it's unlikely he had anything to do with the disappearance of Miss Ostrano. Unless . . .?"

I bristled. "Unless what?"

"Unless she met him halfway."

I exploded. "My God, man, that's ridiculous! She hated him. She was afraid of him. Why do you think she came to live with me?"

"Sir, if you'll just calm down for a moment I'll explain something. In many cases like this we find there was no kidnapping, no coercion. The missing person simply left of her own free will."

"Dammit, Sergeant! I know Alaine. She wouldn't do that!"

"It happens, sir."

"Yes, and this is the second time it's happened."

"There you are. That's what I'm telling you."

"You don't understand, Sergeant. This is the second time for Weston. At least, it's the second time I know of. He kidnapped his own daughter. She had left him and was living with me."

Sergeant Haller was looking curiously at me now. I began to feel that I was under suspicion.

"Sir, let me get this straight. Are you telling me that two young women were living with you and both are missing?"

"Not at the same time, Sergeant! What do you think I'm doing, running a harem? I met Weston's daughter last spring. That was when he tried to get me to join his cult. I didn't go for it. Neither did his daughter. And when Weston learned we were seeing each other he tried to break us up. She left him and came to live with me and that was when he took her. I came home one day and she was gone. And let me tell you, Sergeant, he admitted taking her!"

Sergeant Haller seemed more sympathetic now. "Where is his daughter?"

"I don't know. No one knows. We heard one day, Alaine and I, we heard she tried to escape from somewhere, but we didn't know where."

Sergeant Haller was getting up. "I think I'd better have someone get all this down. I'll bring someone in here and you can tell the whole story. Sit tight for a moment, okay?"

You bet I was going to sit tight. I wanted some action and I was going to get it at last. Sergeant Haller returned with a young woman whom he introduced as Officer Petty. She was a pert young officer, very blonde, and very efficient-looking in her blue uniform. I told my story again, in greater detail this time. She took it down, interrupted at times by Sergeant Haller.

"Did Weston mention any other address he had?"

"Not that I recall. But I do remember that on the morning he got the call about his daughter trying to escape, he left and I believe he was back that evening. So she had to be somewhere in this area."

"That's probably true. Any relatives or close friends you know of?"

"No relatives. Joanne said she had none. As for friends, there was the cult. Anyone in that organization could have hid her, both of them."

"Right. Well, John, tell you what I want you to do. Go home and stay there. I mean, you leave Weston to us. Don't go running after him. That's our job, okay?"

"Sure."

"You think he's coming for you, like he said?"

"I don't think so. He wanted Alaine. Now that he's got her, he'll leave me alone. Unless I go after him like before."

"Which is exactly what I don't want you to do. We'll find him and we'll find his daughter and Miss Ostrano."

"Right."

"One more thing. I'm going to give you the address of a Doctor Noia. He is into psychic research. We've used him in the past and had some success. Tell him what you told me. Maybe he can get some vibrations or whatever he uses that will be useful."

"Sure, I'm game."

"You remember what I told you, John. Leave Weston to us. Don't go running off and get yourself hurt."

"I heard you, Sergeant. I wouldn't know where to look anyway."

I didn't, but when I did you can bet I wouldn't be sitting idly by.

Chapter 23

If I had expected to see a comedic ghost buster I could not have been more mistaken. Doctor Noia was about fifty years old and very professional.

"So what is this all about?" he asked.

I had already briefed him when I asked for an appointment. Now I needed to go into detail.

"As I said, there's this man Weston who claims he is a devil called AAI. When I first met him he wanted me to join his cult. That cult has been disbanded, by the way."

"I heard the news report," Noia interrupted to say.

"Yeah, well, Weston escaped and hasn't been found yet. He has a daughter named Joanne. She lived with me for awhile. When Weston found out, he kidnapped her and hid her someplace. She's still missing."

"Did she belong to the cult?"

"She hated it! That's the reason she left. Well, that's one reason."

Noia nodded as if he understood. "Go on."

"I went to Weston's house and demanded to see her. He became abusive and knocked me out with some kind of brain wave. I don't expect you to believe that, but he did. I lost consciousness and when I woke up I had been brainwashed into joining his cult. I also lost all memory of his daughter.

"So I started working for Weston, doing research for his newspaper, and then I met his secretary, Alaine. We got interested in each other and started dating. When Weston found out, he kicked me out of his organization and put Alaine off limits. One night when Weston wasn't home I went to his house, found Alaine, and brought her back to my place. That infuriated Weston. He kidnapped Alaine and I haven't found her either. The police say they can't do anything. They say she might have gone willingly. I know her. She's afraid of Weston. There's no way she would have left unless he forced her."

Noia drummed on a table top with his fingers, "So all three people are missing."

"The police searched his house, but it's empty. They don't know where to look. They think, with your help, with your sixth sense . . ."

"Sergeant Haller spoke to me earlier. He wanted me to talk to you firsthand and feel you out. Get a few vibrations." Noia continued to drum on the table top. "This Weston, what does he look like? Does he have a pointed beard or . . . ?"

"Good Lord, no! He looks no different than you or me. Middle-aged, on the heavy side, if you don't mind my mentioning that. He can be charming at times, very charming. Then again he can be ruthless. Get in his way and watch out. So what do you think? Does any of this make sense? Do you think I'm imagining all of this?"

"No. I don't think you're imagining this. There have been many Westons in the world. Charles Manson is still fresh in our minds. An evil man, a demented mind. He attracted many people, especially young women. They believed in him completely. Was he a devil? We call him that. In actuality, no. He had no demonic powers. There is a dark side in all of us and it is attracted to evil. Some of us succumb to this fascination and we join cults and follow leaders with unusual beliefs. We call these people fanatics. The Middle Ages is full of stories of men and women, even monks, who delved into the occult, claimed satanic powers, and attracted followers. Then there were people like Vlad the Impaler or Sawney Beane and his family who practiced cannibalism in early Scotland. These people committed horrible crimes. Despicable people, scum of the earth. Devils? Spawns of hell? No.

"But demons by possession? We believe that is possible because the Bible mentions it. If we read the history of the Inquisition we find many cases of accused victims. Even nuns. Especially nuns. In sixteenth-century Spain nuns were reported to bleat like sheep, tear off their veils, have convulsions in church. In seventeenth-century Lyon fifty nuns were afflicted with mass hysteria. In Vienna a nineteen-year-old girl suffered from cramps and was considered demoniac. Jesuits expelled over 10,000 devils. And so on.

"Now take this man Weston. He was born normal as you and me. Sometime in his life something may have happened, a disappointment, a tragedy . . ."

"His wife died a few years ago," I said. "His daughter mentioned that it affected him deeply."

"Good example. So here he is, deeply depressed, furious maybe at the doctors who couldn't save her life, maybe cursing God to whom he prayed and who ignored his pleas. Now he is a sitting duck for the devil to come in and take over. And when I say 'take over' I mean exactly that. At first the mind accepts suggestions of the devil. Gradually the devil takes over the body and the devil becomes the man. You say Weston has demonic powers? That means the possession may already be taking place. We must stop him before the transformation is complete."

Chapter 24

Demonism, satanic rituals, romantic entanglements, voodoo, mystery, terror, and now paranormal activity. What a turn of events my life had taken. For one who had expected nothing more of life than to make a decent living, perhaps marry and settle down to a happy family existence, things had gotten completely out of hand.

If I had never taken that job at Smith and Holmes, if I had never met Weston, if I had never agreed to visit with him, if I had never met his daughter—so many ifs, so many paths I had taken, so many fateful circumstances had led me astray.

The only feelings I had ever experienced were of satisfaction, contentment, expectation, friendship. Now I was filled with hate, despair, anger, revenge—feelings that, if uncontrolled, could lead me down a dangerous road.

What Noia proposed was to go to Weston's house and try to pick up anything that might be helpful. He planned to go alone, believing the presence of others would be distracting. I objected. I was deeply involved in this affair and deserved a shot at determining the outcome. Reluctantly, he agreed, with the provision that Haller should never know. What neither of us knew was that what we were doing was dangerous and could put us in peril of our lives.

We chose early evening. Although Weston's house was somewhat secluded it seemed less likely that we would be noticed at that time. We had no trouble entering. Noia had a passkey. A flood of memories hit me as we stepped into the hallway. I had known happy times here, the dinner that first evening when I met Joanne, the days working with Alaine. But my hatred for Weston overwhelmed all of that.

"A lot of hatred in this house," Noia remarked immediately. "I can feel it."

"You got that right," I agreed.

I led him into the room where Alaine and I had worked. Everything seemed the same as before. I pictured Alaine sitting at her desk, flashing that wonderful smile.

"Anger," Noia murmured. "Lots of anger in this room. I have a strong sense of confrontation, of heated feelings..."

"Sure. We argued here. Weston was furious because I was dating Alaine and he believed I was turning her against him and the cult. This is where he threw me out. He warned me to keep away from her or he'd kill me."

"He actually said he'd kill you?"

"Well, he said I was dead if I tried to contact her. I guess that's what he meant."

"That anger is still here. It's very strong."

Noia moved about the room, touching Alaine's desk, her typewriter, pens, and pencils. He was alone in his thoughts, looking, sensing, probing.

"Picking up anything?" I asked.

He didn't answer. He was in his own world. He wouldn't have heard me unless I yelled.

"Let's see the rest of the house," he said abruptly.

I had seen some of the rest of the house, the dining room, kitchen, and bath. Two spare bedrooms and the garage made up the rest of the downstairs. We looked in all of them, but if Noia learned anything he kept it to himself.

We ascended the stairs to the second floor. Noia seemed attracted to the railing, rubbing his hand over it several times as we went up. Was he sensing something or merely enjoying the feel of the wood? The second floor held eight rooms. The first we entered had been Alaine's. I remembered how happy she had been to see me that last night here, how hurriedly she had packed and how we had wanted to avoid meeting Weston. Noia touched everything, the bed, the dresser, curtains, pictures. He looked into drawers and closets. He kept all observations to himself.

The next room had been Weston's. I suspect it surprised Noia as much as it did me. There were feminine touches everywhere, at the windows, on the bed, the light fixtures, everything. This was a woman's room. She had planned and decorated it and had her way with everything. Clearly Weston had loved his wife dearly. He had continued to sleep here and apparently in her memory had not changed a thing.

Surely Noia would learn something here. He inspected everything, touched everything. At times he paused as if to look and listen, eyes closed into slits, shutting me out, shutting out everything except the vibrations he hoped to feel.

"There's much here," he muttered to himself. "Too much. It's all muddled, confused. I can't sort it out. We must look further."

He headed for the door.

The six remaining rooms were sparsely furnished, save one. This had been Joanne's. Her picture was on the dresser.

Did my heart beat wildly? Did my soul cry out to her? Was it she who was foremost in my mind? If Noia was confused, my mind was in turmoil. I wanted to take her picture and clasp it to my breast. I resisted the urge. Hadn't I committed myself to Alaine? How could I be in love with both of them?

"Yes," Noia murmured, "this is the daughter's room. This is where she rebelled against her father. Much tension here . . . a lot of anger . . ."

We lingered a little longer while Noia played out his role. If he was a fraud, if all his touching and posing were for my benefit, I was impressed. But what did he hope to gain from it? My approval meant nothing.

We went back downstairs. Again the railing got his attention, I suspected it was more than a passing interest in the wood.

In the library Noia became more animated. He paced back and forth between Alaine's desk and the door, shaking his right forefinger in the air as if making a point, then laying it aside his nose.

"Here in this room the drama unfolded . . . Yes, I'm sure of it . . . she stood by the desk . . . and he threatened her . . . she was crying . . . resisting him . . ."

I had never thought a man as large as Noia could become so animated. He was saying words that weren't his.

"'You defy me, Alaine? You were given to me! Yes, you! Who do you think you are to reject me? I can destroy you with a flick of my finger.'"

"'No! No!'"

"'Yes, Alaine, now you know the truth. You were promised to me, my pact with Lucifer. You in exchange for my body, my soul.'"

"'O, Holy Mary!'"

"'Praying, Alaine? It's too late for praying! You've given yourself to me. If I go to hell, you go also!'"

"She ran from the room . . . He tried to stop her . . . the rail!"

Noia himself ran from the room. I found him at the foot of the stairs, running his hand over the wood.

"She went for the stairs . . . tried to escape . . . the railing . . . the railing . . . Aargh!"

Noia fell backward as if he had been shot. He was clutching his left hand.

Did I imagine it? Was the railing beginning to glow?

"She let go . . ." Noia was babbling again, "she had to . . . she fell . . . unconscious . . ." Suddenly Noia lunged for the door.

"C'mon!" he yelled over his shoulder. "I know where she is!"

Chapter 25

I should have guessed. Of course Weston would take her there. It was his temple, his sanctuary. The authorities had raided it and rounded up members of the cult but the house remained intact and empty. After a time what few police were in this unincorporated part of the county had devoted their time and attention elsewhere. What happened to the original owners was anybody's guess.

Weston could come here, hide out for weeks, months, as long as it took him to get his act together, and as long as he remained inconspicuous and caused no disturbance.

The place was isolated, set on a road seldom traveled. Unless the house was put up for sale, it was unlikely to have any visitors, except for curiosity seekers and looters.

I remembered the house, but I had no idea of how to get there. Noia knew. Perhaps he had gotten the information from Haller earlier. Those two had apparently discussed this case more than I realized.

When we pulled up in the yard, memories of those nights of horror came rushing back. Here it was I had gotten my first look at the cult, saw the depravity in devil worship, saw Alaine become a willing proselyte. For what? For an idiotic belief that Satan ruled the world? That free choice was man's birthright, the right to do as one pleased and hang the consequences? Here it was too that I had known Weston's wrath and fell victim to that strange power he had to sway minds and alter beliefs.

Alaine, was she here in this house, a prisoner? Or had she succumbed once more to Weston and become a willing partner? And what of Joanne? Joanne, whom Weston intended to be high priestess of his cult. Was she here? If she was, what devilish plan was Weston concocting for her?

Then there was Noia. If he was so sure we would find Weston here why didn't he inform the police and let them handle it? Surely that was Haller's intention. Weston was a dangerous man. Why put ourselves at risk by coming here alone and unprotected? If we stumbled upon Weston there was no telling what that evil genius might do.

So I had misgivings about entering, but Noia used his passkey and I followed him inside. The house had been full of people previously. Now it was silent. Silent and eerie. I was no psychic but I had a strong sense of dread here. This was a house that had turned to evil and it resented any intruders. It was warning us to get out and leave it alone. We weren't welcome here.

I stayed close to Noia as we entered the living room. I had a silly notion that his bulk would protect me. That would be a vain hope where Weston was concerned; his powers were more than physical.

"What do you think?" I asked. "Think they're all here?"

"They're here," Noia answered. "We're going to have to be extremely careful. No telling what the man is up to."

So why don't we leave? I wanted to ask. Aren't we crazy coming here?

My scalp began to tingle. My hair stood on end.

"What the . . ." I muttered. "What's going on?"

"Shhh!" Noia whispered. "Stand still. It's a probe. Weston knows we're here. He's trying to find out who we are."

The air seemed electrified. There was a burning smell to it and it made my skin sting. For a moment. Then the sensation ended.

"Is it over?" I whispered. "That was eerie."

"For now. No harm done. This Weston is good, very good. He knows who we are and why we're here. Now we can expect some kind of greeting."

That prickly sensation had been greeting enough for me. "So what do we do? Aren't we helpless against him?"

Noia disagreed. "We're not helpless. His strength is playing upon our fears. Remember that anything you see or hear is imagination. It's all in our minds."

"That smell wasn't imagination," I dissented.

"No, it wasn't." Noia offered no explanation. Perhaps he had none.

We went from room to room. Everything seemed normal, everything except that ominous air of evil. The house reeked of it.

"The basement," Noia said.

The basement is where I didn't want to go. If Weston was in the house, the basement is where he would be.

I dreaded opening the door. We could be descending into hell.

Noia turned the knob and pushed. About a dozen steps led downward, lit by an overhead bulb. All seemed normal. No one appeared to challenge us. Noia gave a little grunt of satisfaction or determination and took one step down. His huge body blocked the doorway.

Then I heard him gasp. His head and shoulders fell and he lunged backward, trying to retreat.

Whoosh!

A ball of fire flashed past his head, leaving a trail of sparks behind it. It dashed against the opposite wall and erupted in a blaze of pyrotechnics before falling harmlessly to the floor.

"What was that?" I yelled.

Noia was visibly shaken. He pulled out a handkerchief and wiped his forehead.

"That," he said, "was our greeting."

"Then let's get out of here!" I urged. "We're in over our heads."

Noia put away his handkerchief before answering.

"Remember what I told you. It's all imagination. We see what Weston wants us to see. Look at the wall. There's no fire, not even a mark."

"But we both saw it!"

"Of course. Entire crowds can be made to see what isn't there. Visitations, miracles, magic shows. It's mind control, mind distortion."

"I still think we ought to leave," I protested.

"You want to see Alaine again? You want to find Joanne? We can't leave now."

"Shouldn't we let the police handle it? We know Weston is here. Let the police take over."

"The police would be powerless here. What use are guns against satanic forces? You can stay, John, or come with me, as you please. I'm continuing on. This is a true psychic phenomenon, a-once-in-a-lifetime experience, and I'm not letting it pass."

What could I do but acquiesce? I was no hero, but I didn't want to be branded a coward.

"Well, okay."

"Just stick with me, John. You'll be all right. Just remember, what you see may not be real."

That was small comfort when imagination can be more frightening than reality. I followed him down the stairs.

I remembered little of the basement. We kept our eyes open wide, expecting anything, but nothing appeared, nothing happened. The opposite wall held a door. We headed for that. I dreaded what might be behind it. Would it look the same, the same semicircle of seats, the dais with red drapes? What might we find behind those drapes?

Noia laid a hand on the latch and lifted it. Surprisingly, the door was free and Noia pushed it back.

Weston stood before us, wearing his fatuous smile.

"Welcome, my friends!" He beamed. "Come inside. I have been expecting you."

Chapter 26

How I longed to punch his fat face until it could take no more. I longed to wrap my fingers about his flabby neck and squeeze the truth out of him. "Where is Alaine? Where is Joanne?"

I restrained myself. I had threatened Weston before and gotten nowhere. The man was unflappable, and here on his turf what chance did I have? I followed him into the chamber and for now at least I would let events take their course.

He was apparently alone.

"Come, come," he urged. "I mean you no harm. John, it's good to see you again. How have you been? Well, I trust?"

I had no time to answer. He turned to my companion.

"And you, sir?" he wanted to know. "You are . . . ?"

"I'm Professor Noia, head of psychic research at Center University."

"Oh, yes," Weston said. "I am aware of your work, Professor. I don't agree with all of your theories, but they are very interesting nevertheless. I'm pleased to meet you."

I couldn't believe Noia actually took his hand. Shake hands with the devil?

"Cut the crap, Weston!" I blurted out. "Where's Alaine? Where's Joanne?"

"Easy, my boy, easy." That fat smile was all over his face. "All in good time. You should learn to control yourself, John."

I was under control, but wasn't it time for action? Enough of this small talk.

"Let's discuss this rationally," Weston went on. "We're sensible human beings, aren't we? John, I know where you stand. You would destroy me. You tried to destroy me, but you see, I survived. You're a mere boy. What do you know of heaven and hell? Heaven is your Eden, your Paradise. After death what do you expect? Life among the stars, life in some Happy Place, sitting on clouds with wings on your back, angels playing harps, singing 'Hosanna to the Lord!' Saints all around, and Almighty God on His throne, embracing all of you.

"Is this your reward for a life of struggle and suffering? Is this how you hope to spend your eternity? Consider it, my boy. Kneeling forever, frozen in time, like some statue, like a block of marble, one thought only, one emotion only, 'Praise to ye, O Lord! All glory now and forever!' This is your heaven, John. This is what your priests are promising you."

"And hell, John, do you believe in hell? Hades, Charon, Erebus, Styx, the underworld, the bottomless pit, fires that burn but do not consume, Lucifer and his cohorts, el Diable, your tormentors, your inquisitors. You'll suffer pain and agony without relief, without redemption, without end. You'll lose all perception of who you are and where you are. You'll wither and rot and decay until you are no longer food for worms, and then it will begin all over again. Damnation is forever, the agony is forever. You'll embrace and shun it at the same time, until in some far, far reach of unending existence all lunacy and madness is behind you and there is nothing left but the torment and insensibility.

"This is your reward, John, if you lie, cheat, steal, rape, murder. Your God decided this, the God you worship, the God who loves you and protects you, God who . . ."

"Cut it!" I roared. "I didn't come here for another of your sermons. Save it for the idiots who fall for your crap."

"I understand your anger, John. Surely I do. But put yourself in my position. I took you in as a friend. I would have embraced you as a son. I offered you a place in my society. What did you do? You turned against me, you turned my own daughter against me. Would you have me accept that?

"But I am trying to forgive. I'm willing to forget our past differences. I hoped we could negotiate, settle our disagreements. But no, you came here with a chip on your shoulder."

"I came here to find Alaine. And Joanne," I interrupted. "I don't give a damn about you. I hope you rot in that hell you love. It's where you belong."

"Easy now." Weston was losing his patience. "Remember whom you're talking to. I don't want to harm you. I never wanted to harm you."

Noia meanwhile had been silent, unable to get a word in. Now he edged between us, intending to prevent any conflict.

"As you say, sir," he interrupted to say, "let's try to settle this peacefully. John here has been telling me a little about you. I am anxious to hear more. I understand you have some communication with a devil. I believe you call him AAI. Who is this AAI? Does he reveal himself? Do you ever see him?"

"AAI is a devil of the First Hierarchy," Weston explained. "He is of the aerial variety. He lives in the air around us and can descend into hell. He is bound by the laws of hell. Do I ever see him? No, although at times he can be seen. Better than that, he can live in man. You see his activities every day in the news—murder, rape, terrorism, crimes of passion, greed, and lust. The people who commit these crimes are unaware of the devil inside them."

"And you, sir?" Noia asked. "Do you believe there is a devil inside of you?"

"I do the work of my master."

"And if he commands you to murder, would you do it?" Noia wanted to know.

"If I am commanded, I obey."

"But aren't you forgetting what you described to John a few minutes ago? Are you willing to accept the punishment of hell?"

"I accept the rewards of my master," Weston insisted.

"And your master . . . ?"

"My master resides in hell. I don't kowtow to some white-robed God who wants us to live by His namby-pamby rules."

"I don't envy your decision," Noia said "What do you expect to get from this master of yours? What can he offer that would be worth the pain of hell?"

"What I want, I will get. That's what my reward will be."

I interrupted. "Well, you haven't gotten very much so far, have you, Weston?" I sneered. "Here you are, holed up in this place, your house gone, your family broken up, the police out looking for you. Oh, you've been rewarded by your master!"

That inscrutable face reddened, and I suspect his fists clenched as well.

"That was round one, John. I bide my time."

Noia was determined to get some answers. "So what do you want from life? Is it wealth and power? Are you seeking revenge?"

"I want what every man wants."

"And that is?"

"Respect, contentment, a good life for myself and daughter. Revenge? Yes, I want revenge. I want to tell my God, 'You abandoned me. I appealed to you, I prayed, I begged.' What did I get? Nothing. He ignored me. He deserted me. What do I want? I want to see a world where God is no more. Man is king. Man rules the earth. This God calls Himself the protector of man. When if ever does He protect man? People are dying every day in wars, crimes, freaks of nature, disease, hunger. Where is the protection He promises?"

"And you believe the devil has more to offer?" Noia persisted. "Will he protect you in an earthquake? Will he rescue your daughter if she is being raped?"

"The master will provide."

Noia would not let go. "And when your life is over?"

Weston set his jaw grimly. "My day on earth will never end."

"Never end?" Noia was dumbfounded. "Sir, what are you saying? Are you telling me you expect to live forever?"

"My immortality is assured."

Noia was struggling to grasp that remark. "Mr. Weston, are you talking about eternal life?"

"I'm talking about immortal life in this world," Weston insisted. "I have no desire to go to hell or heaven."

Noia turned to look at me. I was as stunned as he was. Live forever? Like Cain, to 'wander across the earth until the end of time?

"Sir," Noia continued his probing, "I've been following you up to this point. Now I'm a little confused. Are you saying you don't expect to die, that you will live on and on until world's end?"

"It is guaranteed," Weston said flatly.

"Hogwash!" I snorted.

Noia gave me a look to suggest I stuff my remarks.

"Do you have a pact with the devil?" he asked. "What did you promise for your immortality? Your soul? My God, man, the devil has more souls than he knows what to do with. I believe you are under some delusion here. Do you expect to remain young forever? Healthy forever? Picture yourself after 100 years, after 500 years. Blind, surely, deaf, certainly, infirm. All your friends and relatives long gone. The entire world changed, and probably not to your liking. Pleasures? Excitement? You will have tasted all and everything and you will have become bored with everything. I predict you will long for death and you will not find it. What you will find is a world that grows older and older, and when it dies what will you do? Escape to another world? And when that world dies? Over and over until the entire universe collapses and falls in upon itself, and then it will begin all over again. You want to live through that?"

For the first time I began to see a different Weston. Noia had planted some doubts in his mind, and that confident look was disappearing.

"I believe, sir," Noia had the heart of an inquisitor, "you are creating your own hell on earth."

That remark pressed Weston's button. He had tried to be charming. He had tried to communicate. Noia had blown his fuse.

Now Weston exploded. "You speak of hell? You want to see hell? I can give you hell! I can make you wish you had never heard of hell or demons!"

He thrust out his right arm and flourished it. The basement shuddered to a roar of thunder and beastly clamor.

The next moment hell opened up.

Chapter 27

They were many, uncountable numbers of demons, all around us, filling the basement. Not of flesh and blood, not of any earthly shapes. How can I describe them? How do you describe vapors, fumes, nebulae? How do you describe shapes that flow in and out of substance, like ghostly mists that come and go, like night creatures—now you see them, now you don't? There are no words to describe them. It would have taken the devil himself to do that.

And the noise, the uproar. Screams, screeches, yelling, deafening discord that would soon drive us crazy. There was no coping with it. I clamped my hands to my ears, but the din penetrated the flesh and sent every nerve tingling until it was ready to snap.

I prayed to God for relief. I prayed the clamor would end before insanity took over.

Suddenly it was over. Weston was beaming. A sweep of his hand and the unholy scene had vanished.

Could anyone doubt him now? Was Noia as impressed as I was? Fear not, he had said, all would be hallucination. Nothing would harm us. I looked at him now. He was striving to contain himself, but sweat was running down his forehead and his face was white as paste.

"Aren't we brave nonbelievers?" Weston sneered. "What you saw was piddling stuff. Did your priests ever produce such sights, John? Did your research ever uncover such horror, Professor? You came here for what? To threaten me? To turn me over to the police? I permitted you to come. I was prepared to bargain with you, to resolve our differences. But there is still anger in your heart. You would destroy me still. And you, Professor, you try to deter me with words, with rationalities. I care nothing for your science, sir. My intellect is so far above yours that I could call you an imbecile. I know of things you could never imagine. I know of worlds full of beauty and grandeur, worlds in another universe, another time."

He would have rambled on and on if Noia had not intervened.

"So what?" he asked. "What do you hope to accomplish? What will it get you in the end, this knowledge that you claim is so superior? Here you are, holed up like some criminal."

"Oh, no sir!" Weston contended. "You misjudge me. Hiding out? I can leave anytime I wish. I can go anywhere I choose. Who would touch me? Not you, not the police. I can't be stopped. You ask my purpose? I have one purpose. Destroy the world! It is craven, corrupt, defiled. Only the animals were true inheritors of the earth. They deserve to reclaim it. But unfortunately I can't destroy one without hurting the other."

Where were all my brave boastings now? Where were my hopes of rescuing Alaine and Joanne? Were they even here?

"Where's Alaine?" I shouted. "Where's Joanne?"

"Here, my boy. Both are here. Let me present Alaine."

He clapped his hands and turned to a door of the basement.

How I wanted to see her again! But was it Alaine I wanted to see? She had been uppermost in my thoughts lately, the woman to whom I had pledged my love and life. But it was Joanne, sweet, innocent Joanne, who had been my first love.

I was trembling now. How would I act? Did Alaine still love me? How could I show my love for her if it was Joanne I wanted to see, Joanne whom I still loved?

Alaine entered and the basement brightened immediately, like a flower bursting suddenly into bloom, filling the area with color and perfume. Pert, pretty Alaine, with her dark eyes and flashing smile. I wanted to go to her, but some inner voice held me back. She did not seem her usual self. Not drugged, not hypnotized. She entered cautiously, saw us, approached sheepishly, as if unsure whether it was permitted.

My own emotions were mixed now. Why couldn't I go to her, throw my arms around her and hold her close? We were like lovers meeting after years apart, unsure of each other, wondering if the spark was still there, if we wanted to revive it.

"Alaine," I finally asked, "are you all right? I was worried about you."

She looked to Weston for approval. Had he brainwashed her as he had me? Had she succumbed to his rhetoric?

"Alaine is fine," Weston answered. "Aren't you, Alaine?"

"I'm fine," she said at last. "Really, I am. You needn't have worried about me."

It was obvious Weston had gotten to her. She spoke like a puppet, pulled by his strings.

"I need to talk to her. Alone," I pleaded to Weston.

Weston gave me that uncompromising smile. "Sorry, John. No can do."

"Dammit, Weston!" I objected. "You wanted to settle our differences. On whose terms? You're making all the rules."

"There are no rules. Only limitations."

I clenched my fists and gritted my teeth. "You fat, conniving bastard! You deserve your devil. You're two of a kind. Can't trust either of you."

Before Weston could reply, Alaine bolted to my side and clung to me.

"John!" she whimpered. "Help me! I'm so afraid."

My arms held her. "I know you are, Alaine. We're all afraid of this man. Stay with me. He can't beat our love."

She clasped me even more tightly. I wanted to say more. I wanted to tell her I would fight to the end for her. Weston suddenly moved to my side. A sweep of his left arm struck me across the temples and flung me to the floor like a rag doll. There I lay, hurt and dazed, and I dreaded what would happen next.

Weston grabbed Alaine's left arm and twisted it while spewing out his vilification.

"I warned you, girl. You're mine, understand? You think you can escape again? This time I'm sending you where no one can reach you!"

He shook her loose, and she stood, sobbing, hands to her face. Then he raised his right arm and flourished it.

Alaine disappeared.

Of all the tricks Weston had pulled, of all the demonology he had performed, this was surely the most bizarre. She disappeared! One moment she had stood there, in fear and trembling. The next, gone, vanished, hurled into some world only Weston knew.

In my dazed state I could only stare at the nothingness and wonder what fate was in store for her.

As for Noia, what a protector he had been. He stood there, mouth agape, apparently trying to believe what he had just witnessed. "Any questions, Professor?" Weston scoffed. "Got any tricks up your sleeve? Any ghosts you'd like to rattle? Any apparitions you'd like to scare up?"

Noia could only shake his head. "Most amazing. I'm impressed."

"Then our business here is finished," Weston concluded. "You can leave. I permit you to leave, only because I have no use of you."

What a fiasco our trip had been. What had we earned but the loss of Alaine, this time for good, and no news of Joanne. Except that she was here. And even that knowledge would avail me nothing.

I couldn't fault Noia for any of this. He had tried to be helpful, but found himself over his head. The more one tangled with Weston the more his powers seemed to increase. We were fortunate to be able to leave without further incident.

Noia turned to me, came over to my side and lifted me up.

"Are you all right?" he asked.

I wasn't. My head throbbed and my senses were slow to return. I think I mumbled, "Okay," and tried to stand.

"We'd better go," Noia urged. "There's nothing more we can do here."

No protest from me. Weston ruled the roost. Alaine was gone. As for Joanne, any hope of rescuing her . . .

Then, at the corner of my eyes I saw a white figure entering the basement.

Joanne!

She was walking slowly, hesitantly. The gown she wore suggested she had been sleeping. Half awake now, she was trying to orient herself.

She saw the three of us staring at her and her expression became puzzled. "Father?" she questioned.

What was I to do now? Go to her, see if she remembered me, see if she loved me still? No hero I, for all my previous boasting. Weston had already knocked me aside, and he had strengths against which my puny efforts would be futile. But I had come here with a purpose. I had lost Alaine, but, come what might, I wasn't going to be denied again.

"Joanne!" I yelled. "It's me, John!"

I felt, rather than saw, Weston becoming agitated.

"John?" she repeated, turning to me. She was like a child, confused by all the faces, trying to recognize one or all.

I started toward her. "Yes! You remember, don't you, Joanne?"

I heard a low, guttural rumbling beginning near me. Weston was unleashing his ire.

I wouldn't be denied. I had loved Joanne, and now I knew I still loved her. It had been Joanne all the time. Alaine had been an affair, brought on by circumstances over which I had had no control.

"One step further . . .!" I heard Weston threaten.

There was menace in that threat. I couldn't ignore it. I turned to face him. If anger and hatred could be personified, I was looking at it now.

"I'm warning you!" he hissed.

The man was changing. Or was he? Surely he was! How could I be imagining it? That fat pink face was growing dark, the eyes bulging, the eyes glowering.

"My God!" I thought.

He was becoming the manifestation of evil. His skin had grown leathery, ears pointed, jaws slacked. His clothes were ripping, and scales were developing on his chest and arms.

"He's turning into a monster!" I muttered.

Bellowing noises were coming from his throat. But who was he bellowing at, me or Joanne?

I moved next to her, put an arm around her and pulled her behind me. Small protection I would be if this creature attacked. At the moment he seemed bewildered, as if the changeover had confused his thoughts.

Noia edged close to me as if seeking protection in numbers. What chance did we have? We had no weapons but our fists.

Even under the circumstances I enjoyed having Joanne near me. She was awake now and aware of me. "John?" she murmured. "Is that you?"

"It's me," I whispered. "Don't move, don't speak. I don't want you to get hurt."

She stayed close, and I heard little murmurings of fear and dread.

The transformation seemed complete. Weston was no longer a human being. He had grown to well over seven feet tall. His arms were ape-like, his skin layered with green scales, his face a distortion of animal fury. For a minute longer he lingered there, seeming to gather his thoughts. Then he lumbered in our direction.

Noia was in his path, too frightened to move, too powerless to intervene. The monster brushed his shoulder with a sweep of one giant arm. Noia was flung against the wall of the basement and huddled there in shock and pain.

Now the monster turned to me. He towered above me. The hate Weston had shown was multiplied a hundred times in those bulging eyes. What could I do but cower before him, hiding Joanne behind me.

Claw-like arms reached out for me. I think I dimmed my eyes. Then . . .

Craack! . . . Thud!

A shot!

The monster lurched sideways, trying to keep his balance. That stopped him for a moment. He gathered his strength and started once more for me.

Two more shots! Three! Bullets began piercing that thick skull. I turned to see Haller and two officers emptying their guns. They advanced now and poured bullet after bullet into head and body. Blood was flowing freely from the punctured skin, and the creature staggered back and back until legs could hold him no more and he tumbled to the basement floor.

There the three officers towered over him, ready to fire again if the creature moved. For a moment he lay there, immobile.

Then, in an amazing metamorphosis, scales began falling away, the body shortened, eyes fell back into their sockets, and skin turned pink. Now it was Weston who lay there, his body riddled with bullets.

C. C. Zwick

I heard a scream behind me, and I turned quickly to catch Joanne before she fell to the floor.

Chapter 28

We buried George Weston two days later. It was a sad day for Joanne. She had loved her father, and he had truly loved her. The death of his wife had been a great tragedy from which he never recovered. In his grief, in his despair, he had turned away from God. He believed that God had deserted him, and he felt compelled to release his anger, to voice his contempt of a society that could work such miracles in science and industry but could not ease the suffering of one individual. And where else should he turn but to the Prince of Hatred? Weston was not the first to embrace devil worship, nor would he be the last. One might forgive him for that. But to involve Alaine and his daughter was unconscionable. Perhaps he deserved his fate. We can only hope that God has forgiven him.

Joanne was sole heir to her father's inheritance. Our love remained intact and our relationship had matured somewhat. For the present we decided to go our separate ways. She planned to continue her education, get a degree, perhaps in sociology, and help others less fortunate. My immediate need was to find a steady job and improve my finances. Sometime in the future we planned to marry. We believed our love would survive the test.

As for Alaine, I can never think of her without wondering where she is and how she is. What an incredible ending for her, hurled into oblivion, stranded in some timeless dimension, between heaven and hell, forever lonely, forever crying out to me, forever hoping to escape. At times I think I hear her, and with every ounce of my being I call to her. To no avail. Ironically, she may have attained the immortality Weston had sought for himself.

The cult was finished. Weston had been the leader and now no one was willing or able to revive it. So matters should have ended. But there were still questions to be asked and only one man would have the answers. Joanne and I visited Dr. Noia in his office several evenings later.

He was delighted to see us. "Come in! Come in!" he urged. "John, how are you? No ill effects?"

"A little bruised, doctor, but otherwise okay. You, sir?"

"Same here. A trying experience, a frightening experience, but I wouldn't have missed it for the world."

When we had seated ourselves and gotten comfortable, he was positively beaming.

"So now this has all ended happily for you. Now you can put this unfortunate business behind you and get on with your lives."

"Yes," I agreed, "thanks in no small measure to you. Joanne and I want to thank you for your help. Without it, well . . ."

Noia waved a hand deprecatingly. "Tut, tut. You can thank the police. Sergeant Haller was behind all of this and he deserves most of the credit."

"John has told me all about it," Joanne added. "We can't thank you enough."

"No thanks necessary, Joanne. I regret that I couldn't have been of more help with your father."

Mention of her father and his grim ending left Joanne looking a little uncomfortable. Before the situation could become maudlin Noia quickly turned to me.

"So what can I do for you?" he wanted to know. "I suppose you have questions you'd like to ask?"

"But are there any answers?" I wondered. "This has all been so inconceivable. Did we experience all of this, or was it mostly imagination?"

"I saw what you did, John. But what is it you don't understand?"

How to begin? I had so many questions to ask. "Well, let's start at the beginning. I never wanted anything to do with the cult, but George brainwashed me into joining. How did he do that?"

Noia was quick to answer. "If you will permit me, Joanne, your father began to dabble in demonology after the death of your mother. Perhaps he had some inclinations before, but it became an obsession. The more he grappled with it, the more involved he became, the more abilities he acquired. You see, the devil has many powers, but they are limited to hell. He can only work through man. When he finds a willing subject, he is happy to embrace him, and that person becomes his agent. Eventually, the partnership becomes so close, so joined, in some cases, that they become as one. That was why we needed to find George before he could hurt himself or others. Unfortunately, we were too late."

"So he got me to join the cult," I continued, "but that initiation . . . Did Alaine die, as George said, and come back with that stone from hell?"

"All showmanship, John. She was drugged, as you were. Everything was trickery, exhibitionism for the members. They needed to be kept interested. I sincerely doubt whether any of them believed in the cult or satanism."

"What do you think happened to Alaine?"

"We don't know who she was. The police are making inquiries but they have come up with nothing. Perhaps she was an illegal alien. She met your father, was attracted to him and the cult. Then again, she may have been the devil's pawn, sent to George as his familiar. But then she met you, John, and lost all interest in the cult. George had lost his wife, for a time he had lost you, Joanne, now he was losing Alaine. That was more than he could accept. I believe, in the basement that morning, he was no longer himself. He was trying to be pleasant, even though resentment of everyone and everything was eating him alive. Eventually it consumed him. The devil took complete control.

"What happened to Alaine? John, I wish I knew. I can't explain it. I have heard cases of spontaneous combustion, where people are suddenly consumed by flames, but sudden disappearance, vanishing into thin air? I saw it, and I have yet to accept it. Weston spoke of other worlds, Joanne, of other dimensions. Let us hope she is happy, wherever she is. Surely your father would have wanted that. As for your father, Joanne, you have my deepest sympathy. It is not for us to judge him. Perhaps we should only say he loved your mother too much."

"So now," I said, "at least we know there are devils."

Noia laughed. "Oh, we have always known that. The trouble is, we find it hard to believe in them. We humans can be so contradictory. The Bible tells us there is a heaven and hell. We acknowledge one and ridicule the other. We accept only what is good for us."

So it seemed we had all the answers. That is, all the answers as far as could be determined. But there was one more question I needed to ask, one that Noia could answer or not, as he pleased.

"Doctor," I ventured, "you seem to know a lot about the Bible. What do you think, are there errors in it or not?"

Noia paused for a moment before answering.

"Let me say this. The Bible is the Word of God. It was inspired by Him, but it was written by man. That is the difference.

"I assume you love Joanne very much and want to marry her. You believe she is the girl for you. Suppose you write a poem declaring your love for her, and suppose you mention that her eyes are blue, but they are really brown. Does that make your love any the less truthful? Joanne inspired you but you put the words on paper. Read the Bible for the truths that are in it, because it holds all the information we have about God, and all we will ever know until we cross over to the other side. That is all I can tell you."

It was a better answer than I could have hoped for and I thanked him for sharing it. After some further friendly conversation Joanne and I prepared to depart. Noia wished us well, and we thanked him again and hoped he would attend our wedding.

"Wouldn't miss it for the world," he beamed. "Goodbye and good luck."

Outside, we walked across the pavement to my car. Above us a pale October moon seemed a fitting, eerie ending to this whole affair, stars were glittering crystals in a velvet sky, and a brisk, chill wind gave hints of cold winter days ahead.

But Joanne and I were together, God was in His heaven, and all was right with the world.